Don Pendleton

The Executioner: Vegas Vendetta

CORGI BOOKS
A DIVISION OF TRANSWORLD PUBLISHERS LTD

THE EXECUTIONER:
VEGAS VENDETTA
A CORGI BOOK 0 552 11108 2

First publication in Great Britain

PRINTING HISTORY
Corgi edition published 1973
Corgi edition reissued 1979

This book is set in 11pt Baskerville

Corgi Books are published by Transworld Publishers Ltd,
Century House, 61-63 Uxbridge Road,
Ealing, London, W.5.
Made and printed in Great Britain by
William Collins Sons & Co Ltd, Glasgow

His buddies in Vietnam had called him 'the Executioner' in tribute to his proficiency as a jungle fighter, infiltrator and sniper. He had become a specialist in 'seek and destroy' missions of a personal nature, his nerveless efficiency and cool contempt of death staying with him through numerous penetrations of hostile territories and accounting for more than ninety official kills of enemy bigwigs during his two tours of combat duty in Southeast Asia . . .

But now Mack Bolan was on a different kind of combat tour, a personal vendetta against a terrifying enemy – the perfectly organized crime syndicate of the Mafia . . .

Also by Don Pendleton

THE EXECUTIONER: MIAMI MASSACRE
THE EXECUTIONER: ASSAULT ON SOHO
THE EXECUTIONER: CHICAGO WIPEOUT
THE EXECUTIONER: VEGAS VENDETTA
THE EXECUTIONER: CARIBBEAN KILL
THE EXECUTIONER: CALIFORNIA HIT
THE EXECUTIONER: BOSTON BLITZ
THE EXECUTIONER: WASHINGTON I.O.U.
THE EXECUTIONER: SAN DIEGO SIEGE
THE EXECUTIONER: PANIC ON PHILLY
THE EXECUTIONER: NIGHTMARE IN NEW YORK
THE EXECUTIONER: JERSEY GUNS
THE EXECUTIONER: TEXAS STORM
THE EXECUTIONER: DETROIT DEATHWATCH
THE EXECUTIONER: NEW ORLEANS KNOCKOUT
THE EXECUTIONER: FIREBASE SEATTLE
THE EXECUTIONER: HAWAIIAN HELLGROUND
THE EXECUTIONER: ST LOUIS SHOWDOWN
THE EXECUTIONER: CANADIAN CRISIS
THE EXECUTIONER: COLORADO KILL-ZONE
THE EXECUTIONER: ACAPULCO RAMPAGE
THE EXECUTIONER: DIXIE CONVOY
THE EXECUTIONER: SAVAGE FIRE
THE EXECUTIONER: COMMAND STRIKE
THE EXECUTIONER: CLEVELAND PIPELINE
THE EXECUTIONER: ARIZONA AMBUSH
THE EXECUTIONER: TENNESSEE SMASH
THE EXECUTIONER: MONDAY'S MOB

and published by Corgi Books

Dedication

For Jabbo Jones Junior, and many cherished childhood memories. Carpe diem – finis coronat opus!

PROLOGUE

On a late summer's day in the eastern city of Pittsfield, a bemedalled army sniper fresh from the hells of Vietnam stood at the window of an unoccupied office on an upper floor of a downtown building and fired five rounds from a hi-powered rifle onto the street below. Five shots, five frozen seconds, and five men lay suddenly very dead in front of a loan office on that Pittsfield street.

But this was hardly the action of a berserk war veteran who was running amuck at home. On the evening preceding the slayings, the young soldier had penned this note in his personal journal:

> *It's a perfect drop. I ran my triangulations last night and again this evening. It will be like picking rats out of a barrel. The setup sort of reminds me of the site at Nha Tran. The targets will not have any place to go but down – to the ground. And that's just where I want them . . . I timed out at six seconds on the dry run tonight and that was figuring them to scatter in all directions after the first round. I think I will better that time tomorrow because I do not believe these troops have been under fire before. I will probably be half done before the reaction even begins. Well, we will see. We will see, Pop.*

'Pop' was Sam Bolan, deceased, until very recently an aging steelworker, a man who had labored with his hands all his life to provide for his family: beloved wife Elsa, elder son Mack, 17-year-old Cindy, younger son Johnny, age 14.

'Elder son Mack' had a few days earlier been granted emergency leave to journey home from Vietnam and bury Pop, Mama, and Cindy. Young Johnny lay critically injured from gunshot wounds in a Pittsfield hospital – and it was from his kid brother that Mack Bolan learned the true circumstances of this family tragedy. It was an old, old story, told many times in the big cities of America.

Sam Bolan had been ailing, had lost considerable time on the job, and had never been returned to full duty. The direct result, of course, was a greatly reduced income. And Sam had bills to pay, one of these a relatively modest personal note to a local loan company. But this was not an ordinary loan company and its methods of collection had nothing to do with legal claims and court action. One does not go into court to collect 'vigorish' – the term denoting astronomical and illegal interest rates. Instead, one lies in wait in a dark alley with a baseball bat and smashes the delinquent borrower's shoulder or elbow, or breaks a nose and dislodges several teeth in transmitting the demand for payment. One may also threaten members of the immediate family with bodily harm, urge wives and daughters into prostitution or pressure the borrower into committing theft. All these approaches failing, an astute loanshark might feel driven to a simple act of murder – as an object lesson to others who might be similarly inclined toward an evasion of payment.

Perhaps this is why concerned young Cindy Bolan allowed a local vice figure to 'make dates' for her in a motel room in Pittsfield. For some time earlier, Cindy had been secretly turning over her entire paycheck – a meager $35 per week from a part-time job in a dime store – to retire the loan. But it developed that this amount was barely covering the 'vigorish' and had not begun to dissolve the principle plus past-accumulation of vigorish. So, according to Johnny Bolan, 'She started working for those guys, Mack. She was . . . sellin' her ass. Don't look at me like that, she *was*.' The kid brother was shocked and angered by this discovery, even while understanding her reasons, and his only thought was to 'tell Pop', so that he would 'straighten Cindy out'.

Pop straightened Cindy out. This was the final straw for a proud man already humbled, humiliated and pressured to the breaking point. Sam Bolan picked up a pistol and killed his daughter, his wife, and himself.

Six days before the sniper-slayings on the Pittsfield street, Mack Bolan wrote in his journal: 'Cindy did only what she thought had to be done. In his own mixed-up way, I guess Pop did the same. Can I do any less?'

A journal entry dated one day later reads: 'It looks like I have been fighting the wrong enemy. Why defend a front line 8,000 miles away when the *real* enemy is chewing up everything you love back home?'

Four days later, the following entry appears: 'Okay, I have located and identified the first bunch and I am ready ... The law can't touch them – but *the Executioner* can.'

And he did. Five ticks of a clock, five roars of a heavy rifle, five dead bodies lying in a Pittsfield street. And that was only the beginning. The only possible ending would be written in Bolan's blood. This he became quickly aware of, learning that his victims were part of the international crime syndicate known as *La Cosa Nostra.*

His buddies in Vietnam had called him 'the Executioner' in tribute to his proficiency as a jungle fighter, infiltrator and sniper. He had become a specialist in 'seek and destroy' missions of a personal nature, his nerveless efficiency and cool contempt of death staying with him through numerous penetrations of hostile territories and accounting for more than ninety official kills of enemy bigwigs during his two tours of combat duty in Southeast Asia.

So now this government-trained war machine was on a different kind of combat tour – but the ground-rules remained the same. Seek out and destroy the enemy – one by one, two by two or fifty by fifty, the numbers did not matter. The important thing was to carry the war to the enemy, to put up at least some show of resistance to the creeping inroads of organized crime. They had evidently found the laws of a free society particularly suited to their own manipulation – so Bolan placed himself also above the restrictions of American justice. 'I am not their judge. I am their judgment. I am their executioner.' So saying, he set out to prove it and to bring a taste of jungle hell to these enemies at home.

Thunder and lightning became the trademarks of this stunning one-man army, stealth and cunning and combat ingenuity were his *modus operandi*; the only law, the only goal, his only reason for living was now to *destroy the enemy*. This he did, swiftly and efficiently, in the initial confrontation in his home town of Pittsfield. Along the way he picked up a friend or two and many thousands of enemies. Now sought by the police and hotly pursued by an omniscient and omnipresent enemy, Bolan very quickly learned that this was a war of no ordinary dimensions. The battlefield lay everywhere, the enemy was – potentially – everybody. He was hopelessly outnumbered, and the only certain event in his future seemed to be a bloody death.

But this was a 'jungle' which Bolan was quickly beginning to understand . . . and to master. If he was indeed in his last mile of life, then he was determined to make every step of the way count for something positive in his war on syndicated evil. Adopting the hit-and-fade tactics of the trained jungle fighter, Bolan abruptly faded from the Pittsfield battleground and immediately turned up on the far side of the continent for a blitzkrieg challenge to the DiGeorge Family of Southern California – and this battle raged from the exclusive neighborhoods of Beverly Hills to the rugged coastline of Balboa, spilling across the hot desert sands, into spas and citrus fields until 'the enemy' was reeling in shock and walking with great respect around the shadows and pathways of this inspired warrior.

International death contracts were let, the price on Bolan's head passed the $100,000 figure, and bounty hunters from every street corner in the nation prowled the Executioner's jungle of survival. At the height of this frenetic activity, our man popped up at Miami Beach in the midst of a Costa Nostra summit meeting to show the Capos (bosses) themselves what this business of unending warfare was all about.

Meanwhile Bolan had become an unofficial national hero, and his war was closely followed in the press and other media. That hunted and haunted face became as familiar to the average American in the street as was any movie or television idol – and equally familiar to every police establishment in the nation. In the eyes of the law, this young crusader was a mass murderer and the nation's 'most wanted' man. Many individual policemen were secretly sympathetic to the impossible war being waged by this lone warrior, but the official position throughout the country was 'Get Bolan!'

Moving cautiously through the no-man's-land between the police and the mob, Bolan one day found himself unwillingly aboard a Paris-bound jet, and *the Executioner* became an international police problem. He also quickly became a matter of considerable distress to the international arms of the syndicate, and his sweeps through France and England showed that Bolan's war was not a geographically limited one – his jungle and his war accompanied him wherever he went.

Back home again, he took on the combined families of New York City, disrupted an organization movement referred to as *Costa di tutti Cosi* (Thing of Things – or Big Thing) and he left a mark on the New York mob which could never be forgotten.

The next confrontation was at Chicago, Mob City U.S.A., which Bolan saw as the model city for the Mafia's national intentions. He very effectively demonstrated to the syndicate that they could not get away with it even in their Town of Towns.

In the aftermath of Chicago, the Mafia – or *La Costa Nostra* – has come to the grim realization that Mack Bolan is considerably more than a mere thorn in their side. This once-considered-simple soldier boy has grown into his destiny and is actually threatening to accomplish what the collective police efforts of the nation have failed to do – he is actually destroying the organization – piece by piece, arm by arm, family by family. He walks among them seemingly at will, undetected until he chooses otherwise and with apparent impunity. He sits down with them at their councils, participates in their planning, insidiously pits family against family and arm against arm; he destroys, disrupts, and demoralizes this previously omnipotent kingdom of evil wherever his attention is focused upon it.

As this present chapter of the Bolan story opens, the organized crime syndicate is attempting to martial its forces for a massive counterblow to end the Bolan menace once and for all. Enraged and embarrassed by the memories of New York and Chicago, the full resources of this power combine, which has been called 'the invisible second government of America', are being focused into the big blow to 'squash this Bolan!'

For many members of the organization, also, 'getting Bolan' has become a personal obsession that transcends any ordinary sense of dedication or loyalty to the brotherhood. For two men in particular, 'getting Bolan' has become more important than life itself. The Talifero brothers, Pat and Mike, have made this vow to each other: 'We will have no happiness, no rest, and no life until we have washed our hands in Bolan's blood.'

This is a vow to the death, Sicilian style. It is the Big Vendetta, and its partners are the two most feared men inside *La Cosa Nostra*; they are the lord high enforcers of the national governing council, *La Commissione*. They have met Bolan once, and failed ignominiously. It is not their intention to fail again, and fate has set their course for the *Vegas Vendetta*.

Mack Bolan, on the other hand . . .

CHAPTER ONE

FIFTY SECONDS

THE task was simple, and yet tingingly complex. All he had to do was to halt two powerful vehicles, overcome the natural resistance of at least ten heavily-armed Mafia gunners, liberate an awesome shipment of illicit gambling profits, and withdraw along a narrow route of retreat before the base camp reserves could get into the act.

And he had to do it in fifty seconds.

The tall man in the midnight combat suit was Mack Bolan, also know as Mack the Bastard, the Black Blitz, the Executioner, and more often – in one particular segment of American society – 'that fuckin' Bolan!'

He was kneeling in a tumble of rocks on a mountainside between Las Vegas and Lake Mead. Directly ahead of him, but many miles away, the nighttime glow of the fabulous gambling city lent a faint illumination to the western horizon. Overhead a bright desert moon presided over the stillness and draped its soft radiance in patterns of light and shadows across the rugged uplifts of rocky terrain. Bolan was himself a part of that pattern, a black-clad three-dimensional shadow – or perhaps, more correctly, a foreshadowing – of death and destruction and uncompromising warfare.

Barely three hundred yards behind and above him stood the guarded entrance to the armed camp atop the hill, the Vegas 'joint' or hardsite, the mob's desert home away from home and also the collection point for the before-taxes 'skim' from a number of casinos down on the flats. A tireless recon had earlier revealed six hardmen armed with Thompsons patrolling those grounds. Another half-dozen or so had been noted prowling about the two levels of the house itself.

A helicopter had landed up there during Bolan's scouting mission. It carried, according to his reading, a team of accountants and an armed escort for the second leg of the skim transport. But the presence of that chopper had to be taken into Bolan's assault plan – it could be used as a weapon against him. A jeep, also stood at the main gate, ready to roll on an instant's notice. And he had found the tracks of an all-terrain vehicle in the powdered earth on the back side of the hill.

So, sure, it could be a tricky hit – and it would have to be played by the numbers. Quite possibly he would not have even fifty seconds.

A narrow ribbon of blacktop climbed the mountain on the approach from Vegas, then circled about and dropped into the Lake Mead Recreation Area some miles beyond. The private road to the hardsite hairpinned away from the state road in an abrupt climb, then ran straight and level for about one hundred feet before curving into another near-vertical ascent. It was here that Bolan had staked out his ambush point, on the level straightaway. He was positioned about ten feet above the roadway, commanding the terrain from an embankment which also overlooked the point where the private drive curved away from the main road.

Coming out of the hairpin, his targets would have the benefit of the one hundred feet of level approach to the next pull, and they would be revving out of that hairpin for the direct climb to the hilltop. They would in fact, if Bolan knew Mafia wheelmen, be streaking along that straightaway. But he had to meet them here, on the runway, otherwise he might knock them completely off the mountainside and lose them forever. He had come not to *destroy* a quarter-million bucks, but to add them to his own war-chest. So, it was here or nowhere . . . and three hundred short yards from the gate to their fortress.

On the plus side, he had excellent cover and command of the terrain, and his own vehicle was stationed directly below on the main road and poised for the life-or-death withdrawal. A Stoner weapon system – the lightweight fully automatic assault machine-gun which had proven so effective in Vietnam – was suspended by a nylon cord from his shoulders. The drum-fed weapon could deliver 1,000 rounds of 5.56mm ammo per minute. The assault drum carried 150 rounds, certainly enough for this mission, and he carried a standard army .45 Colt on his hip as backup weapon.

Bolan's big punch, though, was a harmless looking fibreglass tube that lay on a rock beside him. It was a use-and-throaway light and anti-tank weapon, or LAW, with all the effectiveness of a bazooka at a range of 400 meters. This shooting gallery was a hell of a lot less than 400 meters.

So okay, sure, for a fifty second hit, the Executioner was ready. If it went by the numbers, great. If not . . . well, Bolan would meet that eventuality in its own time.

And now the moment was approaching, the steady whine of powerful vehicles in laboring ascent assuring him that his intelligence had been accurate and that the skimwagons were right on time.

He pulled the pins to expand the fibreglass tube, then he checked the pop-up sights and hoisted the LAW to his shoulder and lined-up on the runway. And suddenly there they were, a pair of Cadillac limousines glistening in the moonlight and slowing into the hairpin ascent, gearing down for the hard pull into the runway. They were running about a car-length apart as the glow of headlamps swept into the shooting gallery. A muscle in Bolan's jaw tensed and he bent a cool eye into the sights, lining them up at dead center between the first pair of lights. He took a deep breath and let it out slowly, his hand tightening into the firing mechanism atop the tube, and the rocket whooshed away on a long tail of flame and smoke.

The potent little missile flew an unerring beeline to the

approaching vehicle, impacting just beside the hood ornament and punching through into the engine compartment with a thunderous explosion. The car seemed to lift itself off the ground on a column of fire, then it settled in a grotesque slide, sprawling across the road and hunching down like a huge beast kneeling with a mortal wound, the forward section engulfed in flames.

The reaction inside the closely following second vehicle was instantaneous and not a second too soon to avoid a fiery pileup, the big limousine lurching to a rocking halt and the gears meshing into reverse as a Thompson sub at either side began unloading into the rocks from which the assault had been launched.

Meanwhile Bolan had quit that place and was moving swiftly along the shadows of the embankment, the Stoner in his hands and ready to join the war. Without breaking stride he sent a burst through the windshield of the retreating vehicle. The retreat ended – the car arcing abruptly across the roadbed and coming to rest with its tail planted against the mountainside.

A gunner had leapt clear of the second Cadillac and had rolled to one knee. He was trying to stabilize a chattering Thompson in a firetrack on the charging man in black. He never quite made it. Bolan's next burst jerked the guy around like a rubber toy, punching him into a deflated heap at road-center.

The other Thompson briefly challenged the assault from the protected side of the stalled car, but a furious fusillade of 1,000 rounds per minute tore through the vehicle at window level and the duel ended in a death shriek with the sound of disintegrating glass.

Bolan was counting beneath his breath – seconds, not bodies – and he was twenty seconds into the hit when the alarms began sounding from the hardsite.

By the numbers. So far, so good.

The second vehicle was secured, with two dead in the front seat, two dead outside and a groaning man in the rear with the money case. Bolan took the money and a pistol away from the guy, pressed a marksman's medal into his hand in exchange, and tossed the money case onto the road.

'Hit the floor and don't look up,' he coldly advised the wounded survivor. The man readily complied, and Bolan spun to look into the other mess.

A guy was staggering out of the target vehicle with his clothing in flames. Bolan took a step forward then grimaced and quickly sent a mercy burst from the Stoner into the human torch. The guy died quick and clean, liberated from the smouldering chunk of trash that fell to the roadway. Then something tumbled out of a rear door and began twisting about the ground just outside. It was a man, bloodied and still bleeding from a head wound. His hands were tied behind his back and a burnt rope was still coiled about one of his legs. A pantleg was afire, and the guy was feebly trying to smother the blaze with his other leg.

Bolan hurried forward, ripped the burning fabric away from the man and, with hardly a pause, went on beyond him, leaning into the demolished vehicle for a quick look inside.

The two front men were only about half-present, if that much. One had lost his head and a shoulder, the other his chest and adjacent areas, and both corpses were already charred and flaming in the intense heat. Two more bodies were sprawled about the rear section and beginning to ignite.

Bolan wrestled the heated money case clear and quickly backpedalled out of there, aware that the gas tank would go at any moment. The man with the bound hands was groaning with pain and trying to hobble clear on his knees.

Thirty seconds, and the numbers were still in pretty good shape. Excited shouts were just now drifting down from the hardsite and somewhere up there the engine of an automobile coughed into life – the jeep, Bolan guessed.

He grabbed the bound man and dragged him across the road just as the target vehicle erupted into the secondary explosion, sending a towering fireball whoofing into the sky.

The guy was muttering, 'Hell, I don't think I can . . .' Bolan deposited him on the shoulder of the road and hurried down to take possession of the other case of skim.

Forty seconds. He could hear the jeep whining down the steep drive, rapidly closing. But the mission had been completed and the Executioner was ready to fade into the night. The scene of the encounter was brightly lighted now and getting brighter by the moment. As his eyes swept the battle site in a final evaluation they collided with the gaze of the kneeling man, and even through the blood-spatterings there was no mistaking the silent plea being sent his way.

Bolan engaged himself in a microsecond of argument, then he growled, 'You want to go with me?'

In a voice choked with misery the man told him, 'They brought me up here to bury me.'

The guy was in bad shape, and Bolan's timetable had made no allowance for such an encumbrance. He fidgeted and his eyes flashed to the curve ahead, then back to the kneeling man. Then Bolan stopped counting – the fifty seconds were gone, and all the numbers were cancelled.

He dropped the money beside his latest unrequested responsibility and walked slowly up the road. The jeep would be tearing into the curve any second now. The ammo drum of the Stoner responded to his thumping finger with a discouragingly hollow sound, and Bolan had already written it off anyway. He had elected to go with the precision fire and superior stopping power of the heavy .45 Colt at his side; now the autoloader was up and at full arm extension, and Bolan was sighting into the point where the jeep would make its appearance.

And there it was, braking into the curve and fighting against the ninety-degree swing, two guys in front and two in back, each of the rear men holding a Thompson muzzle-up in an entirely businesslike fashion and bracing themselves against the wild swerving of the little vehicle.

Bolan noted all this in the same flashing instant that his finger began its tickling of the hair-pull trigger. It was like a still photo, with the sizzling tracks of the big bullets caught there and preserved in the grotesque scene of leaping flames and broken bodies, the bullets themselves showing up as a line of instantly-sprouting holes in the jeep's windshield and mirrored in the concerned faces behind that glass. He saw the suddenly limp hands release the steering wheel and the wheel itself spinning back to the point of least resistance. Then the front wheels of the vehicle were humping up onto the raised shoulder of the road, the little car becoming airborne and sailing out into the void, disgorging flailing bodies in its flight.

Bolan did not see the jeep touch down again, but he heard it and drew a mental image of an end-over-end tumble down that mountainside as he returned the .45 to its leather and quickly retraced his steps to the hurting man. He hacked the sashcord from the liberated prisoner's wrists and told him, 'We'd better get moving.'

'I don't think I can walk,' the man groaned.

'Legs broken?' Bolan inquired gruffly.

The guy shook his head. 'No. But weak . . . hell, I'm so weak.'

'It's walk or die, soldier,' Bolan snapped. He retrieved the money cases and stepped off into the same direction the jeep had taken, down the mountainside. 'It's downhill all the way, if that's any comfort,' he added, glancing back to see if the guy was following.

He was, but slowly and with difficulty. Bolan scowled and tossed one of the cases down the mountain, then he swung back to wrap an arm about the man's chest.

'Arm over the neck,' he instructed him. 'Come on, dammit, let's shake it.'

The injured man showed his liberator a twisted smile. 'For once we're walking away together,' he panted, letting

Bolan take most of his weight. 'You haven't recognized me, huh?' he mumbled in a moment later as they lurched and slid along the steep incline.

'Mud,' Bolan growled.

'What?'

'Your name is mud, soldier, and so is mine if we haven't cleared this area in another few seconds. So save your breath for what's important.'

'Not mud,' the guy croaked. 'Lyons. I'm Carl Lyons, Bolan.' And with that he passed out and became dead-weight in Bolan's arms.

The tall man in combat black emitted a startled grunt, and let the money case slide away as he hoisted the unconscious figure onto his shoulder.

Someone up there was rolling loaded dice into an executioner's destiny.

He'd come to this mountainside seeking a contribution to his deflated war-chest. It had been a perfect strike, right on the numbers. Then all of a sudden he had lost interest in war-chests and all the skim the mob could throw at him.

So he was walking away with nothing but a half-dead cop on his hands.

The Executioner had no regrets. Loaded dice or no, it had been an entirely worthwhile fifty seconds.

CHAPTER TWO

DIRECTIONS TO THE FRONT

JOE 'the Monster' Stanno had spent twenty years cultivating an image of ferocity. Naturally endowed for the role, Stanno's stubby legs and oversized trunk gave him the appearance of a gorilla – and the perpetually scowling face did nothing to soften the threatening strength of massive chest and shoulders. His reputation for savagery and his almost maniacal homicidal tendencies had assured Joe the Monster a respected position in an organization which was built upon intimidation and violence.

In his early years, Stanno had been a blackjack and brass-knuckles man, a muscle-man for shylockers and protection racketeers in Brooklyn and later in Cleveland, 'progressing' to roles as hit man, bodyguard, and mob enforcer. An Ohio grand jury of the early '60's heard evidence connecting Stanno to sixteen specific acts of murder, twenty-three instances of conspiracy to commit murder and an almost infinite list of assaults and extortion. The jury failed to act on these charges and Stanno abruptly dropped from view. Some time later Joe the Monster turned up in Las Vegas as 'security chief' at the Gold Duster, one of the strip's newest luxury hotels.

Intelligence gleaned by interested federal officals indicated that Stanno's major role at Vegas was that of an inter-family 'enforcer' – and that his line of authority descended directly from *La Commissione*, or the national ruling council of syndicate bosses. It was known that the mob regarded Las Vegas as an open city, meaning only that no *one family* exercised territorial jurisdiction over the underworld action there – the field was open to any and all. Joe the Monster's position was therefore a highly important one; it was his task to see that inter-family rivalries and competitive pursuits were maintained at a peaceful and mutually productive pace. He was, in short, the ruling council's 'man on the scene' and responsible for syndicate discipline throughout the state of Nevada.

None would argue that Joe the Monster Stanno was not the perfect man for the job. His mere presence in any family gathering was enough to calm belligerent moods and soothe aggressive instincts. It had become such a standing joke, in fact, that when disputes arose within the cadre, a peacemaker would warn the belligerents: 'You guys knock it off or I'll call Joe the Monster in here to stare at you.' The jest was not without factual foundation. A mere scowl from Stanno was usually enough to calm the ruffled sensitivities of even high rankholders in the various families.

And now Joe the Monster was standing woodenly in the midst of a disaster area and scowling at the incredible carnage visited upon that mountainside. In the illumination provided by several pairs of vehicle headlamps, a small collection of hardmen from the hilltop retreat prowled the scene with shotguns and Thompson automatics, making a body count, identifying the dead and trying to pull together some understanding of what had transpired there.

A gun-crew chief spun away from the blackened and smoking hulk of a skimwagon and called over, 'It was a heist all right, Joe. There ain't no sign of money. Them boxes was fireproof. And they ain't here.'

Stanno rumbled, 'So where'd it get off to so fast?'

'Jeez I dunno, Joe,' the man called back. 'All I know is they sure made a hard hit. I never saw such a mess.'

'Well I want a headcount!' Stunno yelled. 'I want every goddam man accounted for, and they better damn sure come up with some straight stories!'

'You don't think some of our own boys—'

'Shut up what I think! Don't tell me what I think! Where the hell is Georgie Palazzo and his boys, huh? I don't like the way they just up and disappear, right when all hell is breaking. I wanta know—'

'Down here!' came a cry from the darkness behind Stanno. 'It's Georgie's jeep, tore to hell!'

The enforcer jerked a thumb toward the distant voice and commanded the crewchief, 'Go check it out!'

The head gunner selected two men to accompany him and the three of them disappeared down the mountainside. Another man hurried over to Stanno and announced, 'Sorry, Joe –Tickets just died.'

'You got nothing out of him?' the enforcer rumbled.

The man shook his head. 'Not from his mouth. But he had this in his fist.' He handed over a metallic object and stepped back to a respectful distance.

Stanno hefted the object in an open palm and squintingly inspected it in the harsh light. 'What the hell is that?' he growled.

'That's what you call a marksman's medal,' the hardman replied. 'This was a Bolan hit, Joe.'

'Bolan?' Stunno exploded.

The soldier swallowed nervously and took another retreating step. 'It sure looks like it, Joe. Those things are his business cards, those medals. He always leaves one. I was down in Miami when—'

'Awright awright!' Stanno roared. He exploded into forward motion and swept the gun soldier out of his way as he descended wrathfully upon the wreckage for a personal inspection.

The other soldiers maintained a discreet distance as Joe the Monster plowed through the remains of his skim convoy. Someone muttered, 'Watch it, Joe is pissed.'

The crewchief and his small party reappeared on the roadway and crossed grimly to the other side to make their unhappy report to the boss. Stanno's huge shoulders flexed restlessly as he listened, then he tossed his head back like a jungle ape and bawled, 'Awright, back to th' joint!'

He flung himself away from the wreckage and moved quickly up the road toward his vehicle.

'Don't fuck around with this junk! Shove that stuff off the road and get these dead boys up to the house!' He spun about in mid-stride to jab a quivering finger toward the crewchief. 'Get on the radio and tell that chopper to come on back. That guy is either long gone or he's just hanging around waiting to throw us another punch. But get everybody back to the joint. We're going hard.'

'Going hard!' simply meant a withdrawal into heavy defenses. Joe the Monster had not survived twenty years violence on ferocity alone. He had learned, also, when to pull in his horns and retrench.

And for one split-second there, on that macabre mountain road, he had shown a face to his boys which they had never before seen atop Joe Stanno's beefy shoulders – a face filled with fear and anxiety. Perhaps the old adage is true, the one which suggests that at the heart of every thug lurks an inherent weakness and fear . . . and perhaps even cowardice. Or maybe Joe the Monster was simply a realist with an instinctive respect for the incomprehensible.

One thing seemed certain.

Not even Joe Stanno was willing to blunder about out there at the edge of oblivion with Mack the Bastard on the warpath. Besides, the Talifero brothers – Stanno's direct superiors on *La Commissione* – had a national alert out for this guy. They were demanding immediate notification of any contact with Bolan.

Stanno was only following orders.

Even for a monster man, it seemed the sensible thing to do.

Carl Lyons had first crossed paths with Bolan during the latter's strikes against the Los Angeles based family of Julian DiGeorge, when the young sergeant of detectives was assigned to the special 'get Bolan' detail, code-named *Hardcase*. They had come together in one of those electrifying nose-to-nose encounters at the height of a Bolan hit, and found themselves staring at each other over a pair of hot and ready weapons.

Some hours prior to that confrontation, Bolan had made something of an ass of the young cop during a high speed chase along the Los Angeles freeways, and Lyons had been fairly itching to get another crack at the illusive man in black. And then when the opportunity had come, this tough up-and-coming L.A. cop had simply stood there in frozen amazement and watched the audacious blitz artist sheath his weapon, turn his back, and calmly walk away – after announcing, 'You're not the enemy.'

The worst part, from the detective's point of view, was that he had allowed the most wanted man in Los Angeles to do just that . . . walk away. Their lives became a bit more interwoven after that night, though reluctantly so for Lyons, and this tense 'friendship' had contributed heavily to Bolan's Southern California victory over the mob. It was also directly responsible for the fact that Bolan exited breathing from that battleground, and that was not the sort of debt a man shrugged away. Not a man like Mack Bolan, at any rate.

He deposited his burden on a makeshift bunk in the rear of the 'warwagon' – a Ford Econoline van which Bolan had purchased and outfitted during the New York battles – and which now was backed into the shadows of a narrow blind canyon just off the state road. Lyons regained consciousness as Bolan eased him onto the bunk, and he exerted a feeble resistance until his rescuer commanded, 'Knock it off, Sergeant!'

'What . . . what's the situation!' the L.A. cop asked, sinking weakly back. 'That you, Bolan?'

'Yeah.' It was pitch dark in the little van. Bolan's fingers were delicately probing the other man for wounds. 'Where are you hurt,' he asked gruffly.

'Just from top to bottom,' the cop replied faintly. 'They've been working on me all day.'

'Carefully, I'd say,' Bolan told him. 'You seem to be all here.'

'Yeah. I think they've knocked something loose inside of me, though. I . . . if I don't make it, Bolan . . .'

'You feel that bad' growled the man in black.

'Yeah. I feel that bad,' Lyons groaned.

Bolan had determined that the cop's head wound was no more than a superficial scalp laceration. 'You must be wearing Mafia blood,' he concluded. 'You couldn't have bled all that from this wound.'

Lyons grunted. 'It was gushing at me from every direction. Damn, what a hit.' He groaned again and twisted about in a strong paroxysm of pain. 'Listen to me,' he hissed 'My cover name is Autry . . . James Autry. I'm on loan to the Nevada authorities. You've got to protect that cover, no matter what. Get me? Don't let–'

Bolan brushed aside the plea with a gruff, 'Don't worry. We'll sweat it through. You strong enough to handle a weapon?'

'I guess so. Where are we?'

'Less than a mile from the hardsite,' Bolan replied. 'We're going to make a soft run for it. We just might make it clean if they don't have that chopper up there spotting for them.'

'Listen . . . if it goes sour . . . contact Pete O'Brien in Carson City. Tell him I stuck to the cover story and the thing is still secure from my end. Tell him, Bolan.'

'Sure, I'll tell him,' Bolan promised. 'You think you're bleeding inside?'

'Yeah, I guess so. Listen, tell him it's the California carousel. Remember that. California carousel.'

'Okay. Pete O'Brien, Carson City, California carousel – I've got it.' Bolan was twisting the top from a canteen. He lifted the weakened policeman's head and touched the canteen to his lips. 'Just wet your mouth,' he cautioned. 'Swish it around and spit it out.'

Lyons did so, and a moment later declared, 'I – I'm okay.'

Bolan fed a fresh clip into his .45 and pressed the gun into Lyons' hand. 'She's ready to roar,' he warned him.

'I'm going up front now. We could get into a firefight yet. If you hear someone whistling Yankee Doodle, that's the one you *don't* shoot at.'

Lyons chuckled weakly and said, 'You're always thinking.'

'Until I die,' Bolan assured him, and hurried forward to send the vehicle on its way.

Yeah, Bolan was thinking. He was thinking that all the rotten carcasses on that mountain were not worth one of the gutsy cop's fingers. He'd had his sights on San Francisco, and had stopped off at *funnytown* only to get in on the skim action and appropriate a few bucks for his flattened warchest.

But now he was getting the impression that a lot more was transpiring behind the glitter of Vegas than a bit of lighthanded juggling of casino profits.

As soon as he could get Carl Lyons into competent hands, the Executioner intended to take a look behind that tinsel curtain.

Yeah, the dice were rolling – and from on high, it seemed.

Bolan was not a warrior to disregard directions from offstage.

And, in his combat-conditioned mind, the tussle for tinsel-town was already underway. The Executioner was closing on Vegas.

CHAPTER THREE

BOLAN'S BLOOD

For ten minutes the warwagon ran without lights, nosing quietly along a network of dirt roads and precarious trails, often coasting without power in the descents, halting frequently for a quivering recon of the surrounding terrain.

Not until they had completely quit the heights and rejoined the state road was Bolan satisfied that there was no pursuit. Puzzling over this conclusion, he set a direct course for Vegas and announced to his passenger: 'Looks like we're clear.'

A feeble acknowledgement of the situation came from the rear of the van.

'You okay?' Bolan asked.

'Guess I'll live. And . . . Bolan . . .'

'Yeah?'

'Thanks.'

Bolan smiled and said, 'Sure.'

There was no need for thanks. Bolan knew that. And Lyons knew it. Bolan would have hauled the weakened man out of that mess even if he'd been a total stranger – even if he'd been a *Mafioso*. There was no easy intellectual explanation for this facet of the Executioner's character. As a man given to deep introspection, he often puzzled over this seeming inconsistency of his survival instincts. And he understood only that sometimes – even sometimes in the heat of a firefight – an inner command would cause him to spare a particular life rather than take it. Bolan had long ago learned to trust his instincts, and normally he followed those inner urgings, as he had done back there on that mountain road, even though, at that moment, he had been entertaining the possibility that the prisoner was simply another *Mafioso* being 'disciplined' by his own family. Even though, at that moment, Bolan's longshot for survival was pinned to a very precise game of numbers.

So once again he had followed inner direction, and again it had proved out right. But . . . would it always be so? Could this 'inner command' be nothing more than an inherent and growing weakness, a flaw in the combat character which would eventually destroy him? Could it represent a deeply stirring rebellion against the hell and 'thunderation' which had so characterized his life these past few years? A shrinking from his own fate? . . . A whimpering reach for sweetness, mercy and absolution?

Bolan grunted and flung away the idea. Introspection, a review of one's deeper motivations, was a good thing up to a point. But too much questioning of one's self could send a finely tuned mind into disarray, also – and what greater flaw could there be than that? Hell, he had known what he was getting into when he declared this lousy war . . . he was no greenhorn in this business of impossible warfare, and he'd known that he was renouncing all the good and simple things that made life worthwhile.

He had not, of course, expected to survive this long. He had overestimated the enemy and underestimated his own life expectancy. His last mile, he'd called it – and what a long, grim and bloody trail that last mile had become. What a lonely one. Yeah, that was the worst part – the enforced aloneness, the total isolation from the things that made life good.

He had learned to live with blood and thunder, with constant jeopardy and the ever-present specter of sudden and violent death. If he should live that long, would he ever become accustomed to the role of total outcast? Of course not. And, he realized, he had no right to even expect it. This was part of the price he'd accepted, and this was the 'life' that he would push to the absolute outer limit, to the last staggering step of that final bloody mile.

The life? Wasn't every strike against the enemy a lifetime of its own? Sure. Sure it was. The Executioner had certainly lived more lives than one. And, as part of the tab, he had died many deaths. His first death had been back there in Pittsfield; he'd died first with Mama and Pop and Cindy. He had died again with Chopper and Flower Child, Whispering Death Zitka and Bloodbrother Loudelk and Boom-Boom and Gunsmoke and Deadeye Washington – that fantastic Los Angeles death squad – and he'd lived to die again with Doc Brantzen at Palm Village, with the little *soldada* in Miami and the cute kid who'd become a Mafia turkey in New York. Deaths, yes, very real deaths for some very real and dear people, and deaths of the soul, also, for Mack Bolan. And how many deaths could the soul survive?

And how about those others – the symbolic deaths – those very real lives which Bolan dared not approach again for fear of carrying his plague to them? Johnny Bolan and Val and all the one-life friends he'd picked up and hastily dropped off along that bloody mile of survival – one-lifers who must forever remain in the shadows of Bolan's multi-life form of existence.

Even Lyons . . . even a tough cop like Carl Lyons . . . Lyons had a multi-life existence of his own to worry about.

Bolan sighed and lit a cigarette.

'You want a smoke, Sergeant?' he called back.

'I quit,' came the weak response. 'Haven't you heard that it's hazardous to your health?'

Bolan chuckled. His 'guest' was sounding more like his old self. It would take more than a bit of pummeling around to put down a cop like Carl Lyons. He took a deep drag from the cigarette and sent the smoke toward the rear of the van. 'Lots of things are hazardous to health,' he commented.

Sure, lots of this. War, for example. And trying to cram too many lifetimes into a final, bloody mile of dying.

The enemy blood did not bother Bolan. He *lived* for their blood, and for nothing else. Hell, he was *dying* for it. Intellectualism aside, there was but one way to beat the Mafia, and that was to play their game – their way. Up to a point, of course. The game changed only in those rare moments such as Bolan had experienced back on that mountainside when, during an orgy of bloodletting, he had abandoned his battle plan to drag a dying human back into the ranks of the living.

Uh-huh, and there was the intellectual explanation. It was the name of the game. Beat them with their own methods ... but don't join them. In Bolan's mind, this was the sole differential between himself and his enemies. He was still a human being. How long, he wondered, could he remain so – and continue to play the game? How many more deaths could his rotting soul survive? There would, of course, be one final death ... the one written in his own blood. But ... would the man himself die in the interim? Would his soul depart, somewhere in there, from the onslaught of repeated interim deaths, leaving behind a deranged and half-human jungle beast to prey indiscriminately in an unrestrained exercise of the Mafia game?

Bolan chewed the idea and knew that this was one price he was not willing to pay for his war. Why replace one evil with another? Better to have it end now, tonight, and let his blood and his soul flow out together.

As though sensing his rescuer's thoughts, Carl Lyons spoke up from the darkness of the van and told him, 'You've grown a lot since our first meeting, Bolan. But even with the face job I knew it was you at first glimpse. Or should I say at first *blast*. How the *hell* do you keep it going?'

'It becomes a way of life,' Bolan muttered. Sure. Just commit yourself to unending warfare, then kill quicker and run faster than the other guy. He smiled and asked the cop, 'What do you mean, I've grown?'

Lyons was gingerly sliding into the seat beside Bolan. 'I mean you're not the same wild-ass warrior I faced in L.A. More class, or something.'

Bolan sighed and replied, 'Well, we keep learning, don't we? You feeling that good, to be sitting up here?'

The policeman winced and shifted about, seeking a more comfortable position. 'Not really,' he said. 'But there's some things I guess I have to tell you before you drop me off.'

Bolan nodded his head. 'Fair exchange,' he said.

'You remember the Washington wheel in the Pointer Operation?'

'Harold Brognola,' Bolan replied unemotionally.

'Yeah. He told me he talked to you at Miami. Listen. Washington has an interest in this operation I'm on now. Brognola again. We discussed you briefly during our last contact. He said you made too many waves in New York. And Chicago was the final straw. A congressman from Illinois is really laying the pressure on the Justice Department. A couple of others, too, with plenty of clout. They're saying the FBI is dragging its heels on this deal, that they could've brought you in months ago if they'd really been trying.'

Mildly, Bolan said, 'You're not telling me anything new, and it's costing you too much. Go on back and lie down.'

'No, listen,' Lyons went on raggedly. 'The mob is in high gear, too. They've got a *Bolan watch* on, nationwide – hell, worldwide I guess. Just waiting for you to pop up somewhere. Well, you've popped. This town will be crawling with headhunters before dawn, bet on it.'

'I'd already bet on it,' Bolan told him.

'Double the bets then. The Taliferos are personally leading the head parties.'

'We've met before,' Bolan pointed out.

'You're not the only guy who's learning, you know,' the cop replied. 'Those guys have been sieving through every step of ground you've covered, and licking their own wounds all the way. By now they probably know you better than you know yourself. And they want your blood, Bolan.'

'They'll have to take their place in line,' Bolan replied, scowling.

'Not these guys,' the cop insisted. 'Even a *Capo* walks lightly around the Talifero brothers.'

Bolan's scowl became a faint smile and he said, 'Okay, I'll walk lightly too. Is that all you wanted to tell me?'

'No. Brognola says you can forget his offer.'

'I forgot it a long time ago,'

'The point is, Bolan, he can't even offer you a prayer now. The heat is on and all pots are boiling. Brognola says it's go for broke now, get Bolan. Forget personal feelings and past debts, just *get Bolan*.'

'Is that what you're doing in Vegas?' the Executioner calmly inquired.

'Well no. I'm on something entirely different. But . . . Brognola said. . . .'

Bolan crushed out his cigarette and said, 'Yeah?'

Lyons coughed and clutched at his belly, then said, 'The feds are springing with the Taliferos.'

'What's that mean?'

'They figure the mob's Bolan watch is better than theirs, and they're keying on the Talifero brothers, constant surveillance, phone taps, the whole bit. So when the world rolls over on you, Bolan, your nation's government will be right there stomping the mutilated carcass.'

The man in black shrugged his shoulders and absently reached for another cigarette. 'I've not been expecting exactly the medal of honor,' he said quietly.

'Well . . . you watch it. When the national enforcers hit the scene, the feds will be right behind them – or amongst them. I wanted you to know that. Also, I. . . .'

Bolan lit his cigarette and blew the smoke out the window. 'Also what?'

'Brognola said something else. This, uh, is pretty rotten, Mack. He said – if our paths should cross – I should tell you thanks for past favours. And then I should gun you down.'

Bolan's eyes flicked to his passenger. 'You've got the weapon,' he observed coldly.

'What weapon?' The Colt slipped into the seat between Bolan's legs. 'He said it would be the kindest thing we could do for you. He says you're a dead man, looking for a place to rest in peace. I don't believe that, Bolan.'

'Thanks.'

'I believe you're the livingest son of a bitch I've ever seen. And that's what I want you to know . . . not just because you saved my life back there . . . but because I couldn't have much faith in a world that couldn't make room for a Mack Bolan. Okay?'

'Okay,' Bolan replied, tight-lipped. 'I uh . . . thanks, Lyons.'

'Sure,' Lyons said solemnly. No thanks were necessary, Lyons knew that. And Bolan knew it.

But that familiar tight feeling in the Executioner's chest was beginning to dissolve, and Bolan understood that also. The soul was still intact, and it could still respond to a simple act of human friendship.

'Thanks,' Bolan said again.

'I said sure.'

Bolan chuckled and returned the Colt to his friend the cop. 'These, uh, feds. They're after blood too, eh?'

Lyons sighed. 'Unofficially, I understand, the order is to shoot on sight.'

Bolan frowned at his cigarette and put it out. 'The mad-dog treatment, eh?'

'That's it,' Lyons replied quickly. 'And they'll consider it an act of mercy, if they can get to you first. The Taliferos, my friend, have some hideous programs in mind for you. Need I, uh, say more?'

No, the shadow from the Executioner's other lives needed to say no more. Bolan knew very well what to expect if he should be captured alive by the 'brotherhood of blood.' And the *city of chance* lay just ahead. This would be as good a place as any to face that wriggling finger of fate which Bolan felt crawling through his bloodstream.

The time had come to live again . . . to stride boldly through the valley of death. San Francisco could and would keep. Las Vegas was ready and waiting.

And let all souls beware . . . even the Executioner's own.

CHAPTER FOUR

THE RED CARPET

'HERE's what you do, Joe,' instructed the crisp voice on the long distance telephone hookup. 'First of all, you take every measure to see that our VIP enjoys his stay in your town. That means you attend to every detail. Airlines, buses, trains, private flying outfits, car rental agencies, cabs – anything that moves that he may wish to use, you see to it that he gets first class service. And don't forget to pass the word around to any place within fifty miles that may offer him accomodations, and I mean all the hotels, motels, casinos, clubs, bars, cafes, service stations, everything. Don't let one stone go unturned if it could possibly be used for his comfort. Is it clear?'

'Yes sir, that's pretty clear,' Joe Stanno assured his boss. 'And please tell the commissioners that I'm sure sorry about that slip-up. I mean, sometimes you take every precaution, you know, to extend the proper hospitality, and still a person manages to pop in unexpectedly. We, uh, just didn't have a chance to get a reception ready, that's all.'

'Forget the spilt milk, Joe. Just see to it now that our VIP remains comfortable until the official delegation gets there. You attend to all those little details, eh?'

'Yes sir, I'll see to them personally.'

'Right. And avoid direct contact if it's at all possible. Let's not take any chances on another slip-up. Just keep him comfortable until we arrive.'

'Don't worry,' Stanno replied, 'He'll be comfortable.'

'Fine. Now, I'm sending you some help, so all the highways leading out of that town will be thick with personnel. Any direction he may think of taking out of there in a private car, he'll still get the same warm hospitality. So just worry about your own immediate area, we're taking care of the rest. You have enough local personnel to cover everything, right?'

'Yes sir. I'm tapping into the freelancers just to make sure. Don't worry, there's no place he can touch down in Vegas that he won't be well met.'

'Fine, Joe,' the national enforcer said warmly. 'We're depending on you to handle things until we can get there. One of the commissioners is wondering about that finance team that's visiting you. He wants to know if the project is stymied for sure.'

'For the time being, yeah,' Stanno said, his voice dropping a pitch. 'Our VIP took the deal over clean. I'm sorry I—'

'Don't be sorry, Joe, just be efficient. I'm sure we can persuade your VIP to return the matter to our hands. It would be a shame if we couldn't, though. This commissioner tells me the thing was cleared all the way. It's going to be, uh, embarrassing to have to back out now.'

'Well what's the most important? The deal or the guy? I mean the VIP. What should I be—'

'It's one and the same, isn't it, Joe? Make the guy comfortable, we'll get the deal back. Right? Lose the guy and you lose the deal. Right?'

'Yes sir, I guess that's right,' Stanno muttered. 'Okay. I'm keeping that finance team right close by – I mean standing by . . . you know. If we can turn things back our way again, then we'll be all ready to go as if nothing had ever happened. Right?'

'Right, Joe,' Talifero purred. 'And this commissioner here says somebody had better hope so. He says a quarter-mil is a lot of deal. I think he's right, Joe.'

'Don't worry, so do I,' Stanno quietly agreed. 'Okay. How long before I can expect you?'

'They're getting the plane ready now. Say, uh, about four hours.'

'Great. I'll try to have the thing in good shape by the time you get here.'

'Now dammit, Joe, I didn't tell you to get things in shape by the time I get there. Now did I?'

'No sir,' Joe the Monster growled.

'I told you to see to our VIP's comfort. Now that's all, Joe. I told you to avoid direct contact. Right?'

'Right, Mr. Tal – yes sir, I understand that.'

'Don't get your tail in the air over this busted deal. The big thing is the man himself. Tell me you understand that, Joe.'

'I understand that, sir,' Stanno meekly replied.

A click from the eastern end signaled the close of the conversation. Stanno quietly hung up, his face a mask of cold fury as he turned to his companions.

'I had to eat shit,' he announced in a choked voice. 'That's the first time I – listen, I ain't eating no more.'

'Which one was that?' asked a crewchief. 'Pat or Mike?'

'Who the hell would know?' Stanno growled. 'Look at one, you're looking at both. *Talk* to one, you're talking to both. All I know is, he made me eat shit. And they'll be here about six o'clock.'

The other man took a nervous pull on cigarette and said, 'You mean the brothers are coming here personal?'

'That's what I said!' the Vegas enforcer muttered. 'What's more, we're being invaded. From all directions. They're coming in from everywhere, taking over our action.'

'So whatta we do, Joe?' another chief asked quietly.

'Whatta we *do*?' Stanno showed them a sick smile. 'We do what the brothers *tell* us, that's what we do. They want the town buttoned down – and solid. Thank Christ we're ahead of them on that. Did Ringer get all those calls made?'

'He's still at it, Joe. Want me to check?'

'Yeah, check,' the boss said.

The crew chief hurried out of the room and Stanno went over to a window to peer through a crack in the heavy draperies.

'How do you button down a whole damn desert, though?' he asked in a thick voice. 'I bet that bastard's out there somewheres right now, looking at us through a scope. With a quarter million of the company's bucks to keep him warm. And laughing. How the hell does one guy stay so lucky?'

'I wouldn't call it luck,' the remaining crew chief ventured. 'Not with fourteen bodies laying out down there. I don't think this guy is working alone, Joe. I think he's got hisself a crew. Come to think of it, there might be a whole gang out there looking at us through scopes.'

Stanno made a gargling sound and turned quickly away from the window. 'Let's don't go making things worse'n they might be,' he said.

'He had a crew at L.A. that time,' the gunner pointed out.

'Yeah but I—'

The enforcer broke off to receive the announcement from his returning lieutenant. 'Ringer says he's almost through,' the man reported. He rubbed his chin in a nervous gesture and added, 'How many dead boys did we count, down on the road?'

'All of 'em were dead,' Stanno rumbled. 'Tell Ringer I—'

'Wait a minute, Joe. Ringer's talking to Mr. Apostinni right now. He says – well I only counted ten bodies down there. Is that right?'

Stanno squinted at his crew chief and replied, 'Counting the bits and pieces, yeah, four boys and a bagman in each car. That adds up to ten of *my* fingers. How many of yours?'

'Well, Mr. Apostinni says he was sending out another shipment, besides the finance. He says he was sending us a fink, he says for a termination contract. That would make eleven—'

'Bullshit!' Stanno yelled. 'We don't double up nothing on these finance shipments. He don't go ringing in no terminals at a time like that!'

'He did just the same, Joe. He says it was a urgent—'

'*Bull*shit!' Joe the Monster snatched up the telephone and punched a button to join the conversation on the alternate line. 'Pardon me,' he announced. 'This is Joe Stanno, Mr. Apostinni. What's this you're telling Ringer about a double shipment?'

A smooth but noticeably flustered voice flowed back in a nervous reply. 'That's right, Joe. I know it's irregular but I had too many things on my hands at once here. I've had observers breathing on me all night, and I had to get this other shipment the hell out of here. Now you're saying that this VIP in black has crashed the party, and frankly I don't know what to think now.'

Stanno was raging inwardly over the goddam feds and the goddam ever-present fear of tapped phones and other forms of electronic spying and the constant damned doubletalk on the telephones. Struggling to control the anger in his voice, he said, 'Mr. Apostinni, I don't know what the hell you're saying. What I want you to understand though is just this. We're in one hell of a bind and I ain't got time for polite damn talk. Just exactly what are you telling me?'

The other man sighed and replied, 'I'm telling you we found a fink, Joe, operating right under our noses. We did what we could to straighten him out here, but he just wouldn't straighten out. I sent him out there for you to handle. The men from up north have been here all night, nosing around, asking questions, everything short of an outright bust. I had to get that terminal the hell out of here, Joe. And now I'm wondering just which shipment your blackie was actually after up there. I mean . . .'

'Yes sir, I know what you mean,' Stanno said in a troubled voice.

'What's bothering me, more than the other shipment, is right now this Mr. Fink, Joe. If that guy is on the loose . . .'

Stanno whistled a brief tune then said, 'Well, he is, that's for sure. We didn't find no strange faces in that mess. Chopped up bodies, yeah, heads with nothing under 'em, yeah – but put 'em all together and it's nothing but ten company men all present and accounted for and with none left over. Plus, I might add, four of my own boys from right here.'

'Yes, Ringer was telling me. Well listen, Joe.' The purring voice had dropped to a conspiratorial whisper. 'I realize that the men back east are going to be understandably upset over this financial loss, but listen, what's worrying me the most . . . we entertained Mr. Fink here most all day. I mean, if this guy is a *fed* . . . well, Joe, some things money just can't buy. You know?'

'Yes sir, I know,' Stanno replied heavily. 'Well look, all this means is this. We got to entertain that VIP, right? We do that, everything else might fall back in place too. Right, Mr. Apostinni?'

'You're the expert in that department, Joe. I'll do whatever you say.'

'Then do what Ringer says,' Stanno growled, and hung up.

'Fuck 'em all,' he snarled at his crew chiefs. 'Load up a couple of cars.'

'Where we going, Joe?'

'Where the hell you think? We're going to Vegas. To nail down that red carpet.'

Joe the Monster's 'red carpet' was actually a shroud.

And he meant to personally drape it over Mack Bolan's bleeding body.

CHAPTER FIVE

THE ETHNOLOGIST

COMING upon the Las Vegas Strip, especially at night, is an experience comparable to finding Oz while wandering through the Sahara Desert. Beginning at the south edge of the city, the Strip is a four-mile panoram of hotel-casinos, bars, and motels to stagger and enthrall the first-time visitor, a shimmering neon oasis of glamour and excitement and sexuality that seems to continue into infinity across the wastelands of southern Nevada.

The city itself still shows the evidence of its humbler beginnings; in the year of Mack Bolan's birth, Las Vegas was a rough little desert town of some eight thousand citizens and nowhere equal to the fame and glamour of its sister city to the north, Reno. Now after thirty years of explosive growth, Vegas is a booming metropolis of nearly two hundred thousand year-round residents, and it is a city built and sustained by the state's legalized gambling industry. *Industry* it is. An estimated forty percent of the city's population earn their livings directly from the gambling tables. The annual 'take', or casino winnings, are more than double the annual budget of the State of Nevada, and revenues derived from these earnings provide approximately one-third of all taxes collected by the state. Statewide, tourism-gambling enterprises account for the largest employment category; some twenty million annual visitors leave behind more than $700,000,000 each year.

Las Vegas and its Strip get most of this, with fifteen major resort hotels and some three hundred hotels and motels to accommodate this constant surge and flow of fun-seeking humanity.

Bolan was not overly concerned about 'standing out' in such an environment nor did he have any particular respect for the ability of the mob's local forces to effectively limit his activities there. Later, of course, when the reinforcements began pouring in . . . later there would be plenty of cause for concern. At the moment, Bolan had a quiet and relatively safe chore to perform . . . at the request of an old friend.

Two days earlier he had acquired a room in a modest tourist home at the north edge of the city and had provided himself with 'temporary wheels' – a three-year-old Pontiac convertible purchased at a bargain from a luckless victim of the city's major industry. From this base, the Executioner had scouted the enemy, acquired useful intelligence and launched the strike which had netted him Carl Lyons in lieu of the $250,000 skim shipment he was targeting on.

Now he was sending the convertible into a leisurely foray along the Strip. Dark glasses – practically standard equipment in this part of the world, even at night – and fake sideburns considerably altered his appearance. He wore a light blue suit of the new double-knit stretch fabric. Snuggled to his side beneath the coat was his favored weapon, the hot little 9mm Beretta autoloader he'd acquired while in France, nicely concealed in the snapaway leather, but ready to spring upon demand.

It was 2 a.m. and the Strip was swinging. Just ahead and rising regally from the lesser glow of the neon maze was a dazzling display of electricity and color marking the internationally famous hotel and casino which was Bolan's goal of the moment. Actually the goal was the man on the billboard in letters three feet tall, 'America's hottest comic Tommy Anders' headlining 'the hottest show in town'.

Bolan surrendered the convertible to an eager crew of parking attendants and followed the foot-traffic inside.

The lobby was not what one would expect of a multi-million-dollar hotel. A small registration desk, notably neglected at this hour except for the presence of two sharp-eyed clerks, occupied an inconspicuous spot where the trails diverged – one leading to the three hundred rooms and fifty bungalows clustered about the pool-patio area; another angling off past banked rows of slot machines into the lounge, or bar, where one may sip whiskey at a dollar-ten a serve and play nickel and dime bingo; still another and much broader path led into the casino and beyond to the theatre-dining room.

At a small desk, nearer the door, hovered three men wearing uniforms of the Clark County Sheriff's Department. They were, Bolan knew, off-duty cops retained by the casino for security purposes. Bolan went directly to this desk and laid out the Beretta and an assortment of plasticized cards. 'How's it going?' he asked casually.

'Quiet, sir, very quiet,' replied the deeply-tanned young deputy who seemed to be in charge of the desk. He scrutinized the cards, flashed a glance at Bolan's face, and said, 'Fine, sir. Thanks for checking in.'

Bolan retrieved his cards and returned the Beretta to her leather. 'Anybody else inside?' he asked.

'Two of your people checked in about thirty minutes ago,' the deputy informed him. 'What's up?'

'Routine jazz,' Bolan muttered. 'The weekly jitters, I guess.' He nodded at the other deputies and strode into the casino.

The gambling crowd was relatively thin, a normal condition for this hour of the day with a show in progress in the dining room. Devoid of the casual gamblers, the atmosphere within the casino was tense and decidedly unfunlike. This was the hour of the 'high rollers', as well as the compulsives and the heavy losers trying desperately to get back into the money. Pit bosses roamed restlessly about their areas, chatting with inactive dealers at the no-play tables and hustling shills about to keep up the pretense of activity.

Bolan went on through and presented a card at the entrance to the dining-room. A near-capacity crowd was on hand and completely in the hands of the masterful personality of the man in the spotlight, 'America's hottest comic.'

A harried maitre d' in formal black-tie grimaced at Bolan's card and snapped, 'This is impossible. I haven't a table within opera-glass range of the stage.'

'Forget the table,' Bolan said, and wandered into the sea of diners.

Anders was at stage-center, front, holding a hand-mike and pacing about a small area defined by a red spotlight. Even from this distance Bolan could see the band-aids on his face and a puffy lump beneath one eye. Above and behind him, fanned out like a deck of cards, were the inevitable 'showpieces' – the technically nude, leggy and beautiful chorus girls who typified the Vegas aura of sexuality. They simply stood there like mannequins – living props reflecting the barrage of multi-colored spotlights roaming their sections of the stage.

Bolan stuck to the aisle nearest the wall and went on around and through the doorway leading backstage. It was regular big-theatre back there, with the usual hustle and bustle of activity. A rock group were taking places and getting set up behind a curtain, stagehands were moving energetically about and preparing the next act, half-clad showgirls wandered about, and through it all the amplified Brooklyn accents of Tommy Anders reigned over the delighted reactions from the audience.

Anders had been in the business quite a few years and had always enjoyed a comfortable following. He'd appeared in a couple of minor movies and had recently been popping up on a variety of television shows, but this 'Vegas stand' had, according to the show business reporters, marked the beginning of a whole new era for this 'acknowledged master of stand-up comedy,' a biting satirist who wrote his own monologues, his most famous lines being directed at the sacred cows of America's enthnic sensitivities.

'I'm not no ethnician, but . . .' had become an Anders trade-line, an identity piece which shared honors with his other lead-in, 'Now I'm not anti-ethnic, but . . .'

Bolan, half-Polish, had heard and chuckled over many of the routines . . . and now he was standing in the wings in the reflected glow of a mostly-nude showgirl and listening to the familiar voice declare, 'Now listen, I'm not anti-ethnic, but . . . (pause to allow an anticipatory giggle from the audience) . . . but I hear they're making a new gangbusters movie in Hollywood. You all remember Eliot Ness and The Untouchables. Listen, Ness would get picketed in Hollywood today. Believe it. This new gangbusters flick? The working title is The Unfortunates. They're changing the names of the criminals to protect the producers. That's right, don't laugh. Mike Mazurki has the leading role. He plays a brilliant and brutal FBI agent. Sure. George Raft is the big brains at the Hall of Fuzz, he's the police commissioner. God's truth. Donald O'Connor is the heavy. He's a frustrated song and dance boss who's getting hounded out of his skull by these ratfink feds who keep bugging his rooms and watching him through movie cameras. Yeah, they've got all this illegally-obtained evidence showing the boss feeding LSD to a knocked-up, stoned, fourteen-year-old prostitute. His sister. No, she's not one of the unfortunates. Donald O'Connor is, he's the guy fighting this illegal-evidence game.

'You think I'm kidding. Listen, I hear that Paramount has agreed to change the title of *The Godfather*. They're going to call it *The Stepfather*. A group of militant atheists objected to the use of religious propaganda in an entertainment medium. I'm not kidding I'm not no ethnician.

'Paramount already dropped the word Mafia from the dialogue, and I hear they're giving all the characters Anglo-Saxon names. They're working on the author now,

Mario Puzo. Want 'em to change his name to Marion Push. You laugh, but I'm entirely serious. That's the way it is in America today.

'I was talking to Leonard Slye just the other day. He's been in trouble with the Violence Commissioner. Over his horse. Yeah, you've all heard of the Wonder Horse. Leonard's gotta change the horse's name. Trigger is a violent name, it gives the kids ideas. Leonard changed his own name years ago, of course, to Roy Rogers, you all remember that. Listen, don't laugh, this's no ethnical joke. Image is a very big thing in this country today. It's a matter of freedom, and civil rights and box office. Can you imagine, on your theatre marquee, Leonard Slye and Trigger, the Wonder Horse? Course not. From now on you'll be seeing Roy Rogers and Leonard, the Peaceful Equine.

'There's nothing wrong with that. Nothing wrong with it. It's not anti-ethnic. You ready for the big one? Marion Michael Morrison. Never heard of him? You probably know him as the Duke or as John Wayne. See, that's not ethnic. Even the WASPs do it.

'Image is very important in this country. What looks better on a billboard – Cary Grant or Archibald Leach? Uh-huh. You're getting the idea. It's not a real big deal, is it. It's a matter of image, that's all. Joseph Levitch gets changed to Jerry Lewis. Why not? Who'd pay to see a show with Martin and Levitch, huh?

'It isn't just actors that get their names fixed. Anybody here ever heard of a guy called Sam Goldfish ? Of course not. You know why? Imagine. Metro-Goldfish-Mayer sounds silly, especially with a lion roaring out of the titles. Has anybody caught the smash act just up the street? It's a hubby and wife finger-snapping team, Sidney Leibowitz and Edie Gorme.

'Sure, we all do it. Even the Italians. How many of you haven't heard the great rendition of Lucky Ol' Sun by Frankie LoVecchio, also known as Frankie Laine. Vito Farinola got his name fixed to Vic Damone. But it's not ethnical, it's imagery. This all started a long time before the *Godfath* – pardon me, the *Stepfather*. What's that, sir?'

The comic stepped to the edge of the stage and pretended to be conversing with a man in the audience.

'You represent *who*? The BDBHC. I see. And what did that mean, sir, before it got its name fixed? Oh. "A Better Deal for Broken Home Children." And you object to that new title, *The Stepfather*.'

Anders made a woeful face and returned to his former spot as the audience tittered. 'Things are really getting bad in this country, ladies and gentlemen. It's driving the image-makers nuts. Everybody's getting so sensitive. Open a door for a lady and you get your home picketed by Women's Lib. Have you heard, the emancipated female is now demanding equal rights for names. They say if the kid is coming outta their wombs, it oughta bear their names. I guess that makes sense, come to think of it. But the home run king of the National League, *Geraldine Mays*?

'Listen, this all goes back a long way. A few years ago the black civil rights groups demanded the end of blackface routines. They got it. The industry started hiring black actors for black roles. And that was good. But then several groups started demanding an end to black roles that don't beautify the race. No more gardeners or chauffeurs or houseboys, right – none of that jazz. You think the employment picture in Hollywood is gloomy? You should see the *black* actors weeping, with no more gardeners and houseboys in the scripts.

'Listen, I'm not no ethnician, but . . . the Frito Bandito got shot outta the saddle because the Mexican-Americans got uptight over his accent. What's that they're saying about equal employment opportunities? And the funniest commercial in the history of television – the spicy meat balls gig – proved too spicy for the Italian-American living rooms.

'What's going to happen to this country, ladies and

gentlemen? What's going to become of it when we're all completely and finally sliced up into militant little minority groups all too damned stiff to laugh with each other. Huh? We're going to have to rewrite all the history books. No slave roles, no immigrant roles, no bad Italians or rotten pioneers, no brawling Irishmen or Italian torpedoes or dumb Polacks, no crusty Englishmen or lazy Mexicans . . . what the hell is happening to our country, ladies and gentlemen?'

Anders seemed to have forgotten that he was up there to make the people laugh. He was pitching it to them hard and straight now, and no one was laughing, but Bolan could have heard a pin drop in the center of that huge room.

'We've got to look out for everybody's image, that's the most important job facing us today, it seems. We can't mention Al Capone anymore; it makes the Italian-Americans uncomfortable. In our new history books, he'll go down as Alfred Capingwell, a mischievious little rich kid who was a victim of police brutality. Not *American* police, of course. The "Society for the Image of Good Cops" will have their say about that. We'll blame it on the damned Canadians, they're starting to get pretty snotty with us anyway, we'll make it the damned Mounties what turned poor little Alfie on to bad times.

'What the hell *is* happening to this country, ladies and gentlemen? Listen, I'll tell you what's happening. You think I'm Tommy Andres, right? Wrong. My name is not think I'm Tommy Anders, right? Wrong. My name is not Guiseppe Androsepitone. It's a good Italian name, but somehow it just wouldn't look good on the billboards. You'd think a name like that, though, would give a guy certain privileges in certain segments of our society, wouldn't you? But just a few hours ago, right outside those doors there, I thought I got mugged by a couple of criminal types. All right, let's be honest . . . by a couple of Dignified Dagoes. I've got an imaginary hole up here on my head, and underneath these bandaids are some cuts I dreamed up. This mouse under my eye was caused, I guess, by a sloppy sandman.

'Imagination, all of it. I got non-mugged by two Dignified Dagoes who do not belong to the mythological Mafia . . . and that's the truth. Ask the Attorney General of the United States. He's even forbidden the FBI to use words Mafia and Cosa Nostra in their reports. Ask the Ford Motor Company. They've promised that no television show they sponsor will mention those unmentionable words. Is that rewriting history, or isn't it?

'If it's not, then I got beat up by a myth. This myth laid for me out there in the dark, see, and it jumped me and beat hell out of me for hurting the Italian image. Me, standing up here telling jokes and trying to bring a few smiles – me – I'm hurting the image. These two imaginary torpedoes cruise around wearing brass knuckles and massaging heads with blackjacks, they're *protecting* the image.

'No, that's not funny. I don't blame you for not laughing. I'm not laughing either, even if I got non-mugged by an outfit that doesn't exist because I made the mistake of mentioning something that never was. I can't even laugh about it, and that's got to be the wildest story I ever told, right?

'Well I got some disturbing news for you, ladies and gentlemen. There are worse things than a bad image. There are bad *people*, and they exist no matter what you call 'em or how you try to image 'em, they do exist. You don't erase history by burning books, and you don't do anything about righting the wrongs in this country by pretending that nothing *is* wrong.

'I wanta leave you with one last thought. Awhile ago I asked you, ladies and gentlemen, what the hell is happening to this country. I'll tell you now what's happening. The whole country is losing its guts. That's right. It's gone Hollywood, and that's the truth. We're all so interested in the *image* that we're losing sight of some fundamental and important stuff. I've been telling you for years that I'm no ethnician. That's a damn lie. I'm about as ethnical as a guy can get, and I wanta tell you that I'm not a damned bit ashamed of being Italian. I may not always be *proud*, but I'm never ashamed. What shames me is all these gutless wonders who're *afraid* to be Italian. Or to be Mexican, or Black, or Polish, or whatever else they are. Because that's what America *is*, ladies and gentlemen, it's the freedom to be yourself, whatever that might be.

'But if you still want to sell out to the image-makers, then I got a word of advice for all you white-Anglo-Protestants out there. You'd better start thinking about *your* image. It's getting loused up, and you people better get yourselves organized. You've been sitting around on your duffs laughing about myths, while behind your backs Black has become always Beautiful, Dago is nothing but Dignified, Polacks are forever Polished, and Jehovah's Chosen are emerging as the brains of the country. So you WASPs had better come out of your dream world and get with this image business. Then we'll drive all the image-makers everywhere clear outta their skulls.

'This is Guiseppe Androsepitone proudly saying good night and God bless you. And lookout for the St. Matthews – that's the new mythological name for the Mafia. That is, until Giovanni Battista Montini raises a protest. What? You never heard of Giovanni Battista Montini? Well, would you believe . . . Pope Paul the Sixth?'

The little guy walked off under a standing ovation, evaded a stage director who was trying to steer him back out for a curtain call, and walked rapidly past Bolan toward the dressing rooms.

Following closely through the confusion, Bolan moved into the hallways several paces behind the comic. Two guys who looked as though they had just stepped out of a Silva Thins' commercial were lounging near the dressing room door, their backs against the wall. Anders spotted them, halted, turned about, saw Bolan descending upon him, then he gave a resigned sigh and moved on along the hall.

Bolan was right on his heels when he reached the door. The two hoods started in behind the comic but Bolan got there first. He bounced the first one off to the opposite wall and met the second one with a graveyard gaze. 'Bug off,' he quickly commanded.

Anders was standing just inside the dressing room, his eyes traveling rapidly between the three men in the hallway. The muscleman whom Bolan had unceremoniously shoved out of the action was tugging a leather sap out of his pocket and the other guy was just glaring at Bolan.

The comic gave an unconvincing chuckle and asked, 'What the hell, are you guys fighting over me now?'

The one with the sap took a menacing step forward and told Bolan, 'Butt out, Clyde. You're not needed here.'

Bolan let his coat sag open to reveal the Beretta nestled there. 'Try me,' he suggested.

The second torpedo had been staring curiously into Bolan's face. When he saw the Beretta he gasped, 'Shit, it's *him*!' and made the fatal move, clawing inside his own coat for hardware.

The Beretta broke leather first, whisking out and up and spitting a pencil of flame through the muzzle silencer, a high-impact Parabellum hollow-nose phutting across the arm's length range and splattering through the guy's eye socket with a peculiar sucking sound, the head snapping back and rolling on the shoulders in instantaneous death.

Bolan was holding the dead man erect and showing the other one the muzzle of the Beretta Belle, and the guy was frozen there, his mouth open, horrified eyes riveted to the blood-and-tissue-splattered wall behind his partner.

'Take him,' Bolan snapped, and shoved the limp form on to the survivor.

'T-take him where?' the guy croaked.

'Where to, Anders?' Bolan asked calmly.

The comic scampered through the doorway to peer up and down the empty hall. 'There's an empty dressing room back there,' he yelped. 'God, don't put 'im in mine!'

'Show us,' Bolan commanded.

Anders led the way, the struggling torpedo with his dead burden following closely, Bolan bringing up the rear. They went into a room at the end of the hall and the hood panted, 'What're we doing, f'Christ sake what's going on?'

Bolan ignored the query to ask Anders, 'Are these the boys that muscled you?'

'Yeah, that's them,' the comic replied in a choked voice.

The Beretta whispered without preamble, another Parabellum found mortal flesh and bone, and both *Mafiosi* crumbled to the floor.

'Okay, move,' Bolan told the comic, pushing him out the door and along the hallway.

Anders was wearing a sick look as they re-entered his dressing-room. He went directly to the makeup table and took a pull at a bottle of Jim Beam, then turned to stare dazedly at the tall man in the blue suit. 'Christ!' he said, and repeated it.

Bolan pushed the door shut and told his host, 'It's a friendly visit, Anders. We need a talk.'

'Well wait a damn minute.' The comedian sagged into a chair and passed a shaking hand across his eyes. 'Please don't ever come mad.'

'A man you know as Autry asked me to look in on you. Couldn't do it himself, he's not much better off than the two we just left.'

Anders' head snapped up and he regarded his visitor with new interest. 'What do you mean? What happened to Autry?'

'Someone made a stretcher case out of him,' Bolan replied. 'Your two friends back there, I'd guess.'

'*My* friends?'

'They're sure not mine,' Bolan said.

The shaken man's eyes were searching Bolan's face for a

clue to his puzzle. 'You're not with the mob then,' he quietly declared.

Bolan showed him a sober smile and said, 'Not hardly.' He removed the sunglasses for a moment, then put them back on.

The comic had come halfway out of his chair and a light was kindling in those horrified eyes. 'Oh, hell, don't tell me . . .'

'Call me Frankie,' Bolan suggested. 'Let's cut out. I believe we have things to discuss.'

Anders was giving his caller a fascinated stare. 'You're not a myth, either,' he said quietly.

'I might be if we don't get out of here pretty quick.'

'Hell, my God, Mr. Bolan, I'm not no . . . *Frankie*, I mean. Everybody gets their name fixed, huh. Okay yeah, I got a room here but I know a better place. The Ranger girls gave me a key to their bungalow when these torpedoes started pushing me around. Hey man, you can ride shotgun in my corral any time, and that's no joke.'

Bolan grinned and followed the little guy out of the room. The best stand-up comic in the business was wearing off his shock and the sharp mind was bouncing back for a new stand. They crossed the rear of the stage and cut through the kitchen, heading for the bungalows at the opposite side of the hotel complex. Anders keeping up a quickfire patter of one-liners regarding the mythical reality of violence in contemporary American life.

But Bolan's mind was moving forward to a much more pointed routine from the hottest comic in the land. It was time for a Command Performance, and the audience of one had a life-or-death interest in the newest and unfunniest monologue of the non-ethnologist.

They were going to play a name game.

And the stakes were life . . . or death.

CHAPTER SIX

SHOW TIME

It was a two-bedroom stucco job made to look like an adobe hut, except for the glass front overlooking the pool, with the standard Vegas posh interior and a small combination kitchenette-bar huddled in a corner of the living-room. A hideaway bed was extended and ready for occupancy, taking up much of the living area.

Bolan took a quick walk-through, encountering nothing but an incredible litter of feminine clothing and incidentals. Opened and overflowing suitcases congested both bedrooms, and the both was a hazard area of miniature clotheslines and damp lingerie. Both closets were overflowing with plastic traveling bags stuffed with dresses of every description. Boots, shoes, sandals, sneakers and everything that could be put on a foot were scattered all about the place.

Bolan completed his inspection and found Anders pouring liquids into two glasses at the bar. 'Choice,' the perennial funnyman announced. 'Whiskey and soda, or soda and whiskey. Which will it be?'

'Thanks, neither,' Bolan told him. 'How many of these girl rangers are there, Anders?'

The comedian chuckled and corrected him. 'Ranger Girls,' he said, 'with a capital *R* and a Capital *G* and a yo-ho-ho just to think about 'em. They're really sensational. Four, count 'em, four. Going on the bill tomorrow. They sing, they dance, they tell jokes, and they knock your eyes out.'

Bolan got the feeling the little guy was talking just to drown out his heartbeat.

'Between 'em they also play fifteen musical instruments. They got here early, to catch the competition along the Strip. Old show biz tradition, nobody loves a performer like another performer. Trouble is, most of the clubs show at the same time, so we don't get a chance to catch each other unless we come early or stay late. They're nice kids, Bolan. We've billed together at Miami Beach, Tahoe, San Juan – hell, everywhere. We're friends, though, that's all. They saw me get it, just outside here a few hours ago, and I guess they're all that saved me from a worse beating than I got. They started yelling, the goons took off, the girls pulled me in here and called a doctor. Gave me a key, told me to stay as long as I like, and then went supper-clubbing.' He grinned. 'That's show biz. What else you wanta know?'

'Why're they muscling you? And don't tell me they just don't dig your act.'

'The act I do, I'm lucky I don't get mugged twice a night.'

'You know what I mean.'

Anders sighed and took a long pull at his drink. 'Yeah. The mob. The mythical Mafia. I'll tell you something, Bo – Frankie. If Autry sent you, then you should know also why I'm getting muscled.'

'We weren't able to discuss the fine points. He just said that you're in trouble, something you don't want the cops in on just now.'

'Look . . . I've been fifteen years getting where I'm at, and it's been uphill all the way. If those guys think I'm going to hold still for a death kiss now they're outta their minds. I fought guys like that all my life, grew up on the streets with 'em, and I thought I'd gotten away from all that. But I found out better. There's no getting away from those guys, Bolan, they're like ants at a picnic.'

'What guys? The mob?'

'Yeah, the myths. They've grabbed control of my managers, I've been with ASA since '62 and they've always been a great outfit. But now—'

'ASA?' Bolan queried.

'That's American Show Association. They manage and book talent all over the world, and they've always been one of the best. I find out that one of the partners sold out to the mob. He's working for them now – fronting for them, I guess – drawing a salary. Listen, I'm not—'

'Why worry, Anders? Why should you care who books you, so long as you keep getting the top spots?'

'Look, Bolan, you know better than that. You wanta feed me straight lines though – okay, let's play. You know how it goes. Let the mob get one finger on you, just one, pretty soon they got it clear up your ass and they're turning you wrong-side-out like a dirty sock.'

'Give me a for instance,' Bolan said.

'For instance. Okay, try this one. I've been opening the winter season at the Fountains in Miami Beach every year for the past five. Me'n the management have this thing going, we're like old buddies. Any time I'm passing through I sleep there, and I always get the visiting royalty treatment. It's been that way for five years. Get the picture?'

'I've got it,' Bolan assured him. 'Go on.'

'So this winter an old tradition went to hell. Tommy Anders did not open the season at the Fountains. ASA told me the hotel figured it was time for a change. Okay, it hurt a little, but I bought the story. I go on to San Juan and spend a couple of months playing the islands. Last month I'm coming back through Miami. I stop at the Fountains as usual. No visiting royalty treatment this time, no buddy-buddy at all. I finally corner my old buddy Jake in his office and I ask him what's going on. Then I get the story. You ready?'

Bolan nodded. 'I'm ready.'

'The guy is scared out of his skull. He tells me I can go to hell if I like, but he's not going with me. He says he's not giving the mob one little fingerhold on his place and furthermore he'll do no more booking through ASA. That's hurting him, sure, some of the most popular acts in the business are under ASA management, so I'm stunned, see. I finally pull the story out of Jake. They hit him with this routine, see. He can get Tommy Anders to open his season, sure, but there's certain new conditions now. ASA don't like some of the people the Fountains is doing business with. They don't like his suppliers, especially his booze distributors, and they don't even like the laundry he uses. They give Jake this long list of hotel supply outfits and tell him he's got to use them exclusively if he wants ASA talent in his showbills.

'Well, to make it short, Jake threw them out. And me, of course, with them. *Hell God*, Bolan, I was stunned. I just didn't know what to tell him. I start checking back then, realizing now that I've been putting in an unusual season – my bookings, I mean. I hadn't thought of it before, but these were all new joints I'd been playing. New to me, I mean. So I start asking around. I'm still stunned and can't believe it, see. I even dropped into the fuzz palace in Miami. They got a what they call a Dade County Public Safety Department, it's what they call the Sheriff there. They got this Organized Crime Bureau, and I talked to this guy they call a specialist in organized crime. *Hell God*, what a story this guy gives me, Bolan, ordinary people wouldn't believe it.

'Anyway, I very quick got the picture that was closing in on me. And yeah, they've got their finger clear up into my large intestine by now, I can see that. I been playing nothing but mob joints all season, me and most of the ASA headliners. I don't mean the mob *owns* these joints, not outright, but they're controlling all the action in them.

'Those guys are building a whole new empire around the show business world, and bet your ass – if they're into ASA then they're into other agencies too. And they're building an empire of booze, women, food, vending machines, illegal gambling, services, labor, the whole bit.

This agent in Miami tells me all these businesses on the ASA vendor's list are mob controlled. ASA is using the talent, see, jerks like me, to get that foot in the door for them. And that's not all. I mean, I got a selfish gripe, too.'

'They're selling you down the river,' Bolan commented.

'Right, that's exactly right. There's money in commissions, sure, but that's peanuts now for ASA. They'll barter me into oblivion if it serves their purposes. But that not the scariest part, Bolan. I mean, I'm not all that noble, but there's more involved here than what happened to Tommy Anders. You ready for the biggee?'

Bolan smiled grimly and said, 'Go.'

'ASA has artists in just about every segment of show business. I mean like Broadway, television, movies – when you think of show business, you can't help thinking about ASA, they're that big. Can you imagine what that means? This mythological and invisible second "Government of America" is taking over the show world.'

Bolan said nothing. He lit a cigarette and scowled at the smoke rising toward the ceiling of the bungalow.

After a moment of silence, the comic said, 'You can't buy that, eh?'

'Sure, I buy it,' Bolan replied.

'I know it may not seem very important, but . . . I mean, show biz is just a thin layer of frosting on American life, I realize that, but hell God, Bolan . . . my guts shake every time I think of turning the whole thing over to—'

'I never liked cake without frosting,' Bolan said, abruptly rising to his feet. 'So where do you stand right now with ASA?'

'That's where Autry comes in,' Landers replied. 'I filed a formal complaint with the guild. They sent Autry up to talk to me, and to poke around in the local situation. Said to keep it quiet about this mob stuff until they've had a chance to look into it.'

So that was it, Bolan was thinking. A federal strike

force was probably investigating the thing, using obscure local cops in undercover roles. The term 'California carousel' which Lyons had mentioned was probably the operational code name for the thing.

He asked Anders, 'Did ASA book you here?'

'They did not!' the comic snorted. 'I told those guys to get lost. The guild got me a court injunction allowing me to act as a free agent pending outcome of a suit to dissolve my ASA contract.'

'So now you're getting muscled,' Bolan mused.

'That's the picture,' Anders said. 'Look, let's be honest. I thought I was too big for them to mess with this way. I found out quick. *No* one is that big.'

'But you're still waving this red flag at them all the while.'

'Damn right. I figure that's my only defense now. The more fuss I raise publicly, I figure they'll be that much more reluctant to just haul off and rub me out. I mean, it would be too obvious, wouldn't it?'

Bolan sighed. 'Hell, I don't know,' he said. 'Your best bet I guess, would be to cooperate with Autry. And speaking of that, those two bodies backstage will be found sooner or later. The police will be pulling you in, for questioning if nothing else. When they do, tell them the truth.'

'Hell I wouldn't—'

'Yes you would. Give it to them just exactly the way it happened, and don't worry about fingering me. I'm already on the books as a mass murderer. A couple more won't make any difference. In fact, you'd better be the one to report the deaths, Anders. As soon as you give me what I—'

Bolan stopped talking abruptly and wheeled about in response to a commotion behind him, the Beretta out and swinging into the line-up.

Four of the prettiest intruders he'd ever slapped leather on were frozen there in the open doorway, gaping at the black blaster greeting them from Bolan's fist.

Anders quickly announced, 'It's okay, girls. Get in here and shut that door.'

A wide-eyed blonde at the rear of the group shoved the others forward and quietly closed the door. All four had that dazzling, twenty-karat look that reminds a guy of his manhood, and Bolan was certainly not immune to that sort of thing. But he disciplined his eyes and put away the Beretta as the girls edged on into the room.

There was a hair color for every taste, but the major differences ended right there. They were dressed alike, in peekaboo hotpants and plunging see-through tops which, altogether, revealed seemingly infinite legs and an extra dimension or two in divine developments elsewhere, and Bolan found himself wondering if they needed some sort of license to walk about in public like that.

He showed them his back and growled to Anders, 'Let's get out of here.'

The blonde had come forward and he could feel her eyes measuring him at close range. 'Better not,' she said in a pleasantly modulated voice. 'We just came through the lobby and it's like instant panic back there.'

'I'm not surprised,' Bolan quietly commented, visualizing that flaming foursome leaving a mind-blown wake wherever they passed.

'The girls are okay, Bo – Frankie,' Anders said.

'That's the idea,' Bolan told him. 'They don't need to get involved in this.'

'We're already involved.' The report came from a warm-eyed brunette who joined the crowd at the bar. Her hip bumped against Bolan's and remained there. She smiled at Anders and said, 'I'm glad you took my advice and got a bodyguard, Tommy.'

'Some bodyguard,' the blonde commented. She pulled the dark glasses away from Bolan's face and smiled solemnly at him. 'The panic in the lobby is a fuzzbuzz, cuz. Do you want to hear the rest of it?'

Bolan took back his glasses and dropped them into a pocket. 'Okay,' he said. 'Let's have it.'

'Introductions first,' the blonde replied, smiling. 'Who's the Greek-God-with-gun, Tommy?'

Anders was staring at Bolan with question marks in his eyes.

'She knows,' Bolan growled.

The blonde laughed softly and said, 'Yes, she knows. The Man from Mad, *Mr. My Gun Is Quicker*, and you picked a lousy spot for an execution. There's a blood-splattered hallway just outside Tommy's dressing-room, two dead goons just down the way, and fuzz buzzing all over the place.' She fingered the lapels of Bolan's jacket, adding, 'The deputies are looking for a tall man in a pale blue suit who checked in with casino security credentials.'

'Is that right?' Bolan growled.

'That's right. Those are pretty, blue bloodstains you're wearing, Mr. Grouch.'

Anders chuckled nervously and said, 'Lay off, Toby. The guy saved my life.' To Bolan, he said 'Mack, meet Toby Ranger, Mother Nature's answer to Women's Lib. And don't try to get ahead of her, it's impossible.'

Bolans' face relaxed somewhat and he took the girl's hand. 'Truce,' he suggested.

'Shortest war since Adam and Eve,' she replied, then completed the introductions.

The brunette at Bolan's hip was Georgette Chebleu, French-Canadian, a mischievous-eyed swinger who obviously liked body contact and made no bones about it. The auburn-haired one was a sober-puss with rosepetal skin and eyes that tended to brood; she met Bolan with a frown. She was identified as Smiley Dublin and said nothing to dispute the introduction. The fourth girl was Sally Palmer, a soft brunette with babydoll eyes and that open, ingenuous look of the small-town girl.

All four were tall, sleek, beautiful, and Bolan didn't have to catch their act to know they were good. There was a showbiz aura about them – in their movements, their actions, the way they held themselves – they had the mystique of the showbiz pro who had come and conquered.

'We don't usually run around town dressed this way,' Sally Palmer was explaining, as though it were very important that she do so. 'We just – this is our first Vegas date,' she finished weakly. 'We want to . . . be noticed.'

'Never fear,' Bolan said. He told Anders, 'Give me some other names and I'll be on my way.'

'What names?' the blonde asked, before Anders could open his mouth.

'Buzz off, beautiful,' Bolan said, without looking at her. He was glaring at Anders and thinking how easy it would be to act human with these girls – and how nice it would be. 'Names, Anders,' he snapped.

'Shortest truce since Bonnie and Clyde,' Toby declared. 'Don't tell him a damn thing, Tommy.'

'*Heil God*, you two cut it out,' the comedian growled. He extracted a folded sheet of note paper from his wallet and passed it over the bar to Bolan. 'You'll find it all right here,' he told him. 'My last will and monologue. Keep it, I got copies everywhere.'

Bolan briefly studied the hand-scrawled sheet, grunted, and thrust it into his pocket. 'Okay,' he said. 'Now make that call.'

'What call?' the blonde wanted to know.

'He wants me to report the . . . uh . . . killings,' Anders told her.

'It's a little late for that,' she huffed.

'Better still,' Bolan said, ignoring the girl, 'don't call. Go to the lobby and collar a cop. You're excited, shook-up. I pulled you out of the casino at gunpoint, took you to the parking lot, questioned you, then let you go. Other than eyeballing the killings, that's all you know.'

'Yeah, that's all I know,' Anders muttered. He finished his drink and moved around the end of the bar.

Toby stopped him there. 'Hold it,' she said. 'That takes care of you, but what about Captain Puff here?' Her eyes raked Bolan in a quick inspection. 'Do you also turn invisible?'

'Almost,' Bolan replied, showing her a tight grin. 'Don't worry, I'm leaving.'

'Almost isn't good enough,' she told him. 'You haven't been listening to me. This place is *crawling* with police. I heard them talking. They have the entire place sealed off. And they're starting a room-to-room search. And they *know* whom they're looking for.'

He briefly chewed the information, then asked her, 'So what do you suggest?'

She flashed him a smile and announced, 'It's a quick-change time, girls. Break out the bikinis, the fishnets.' To Bolan, she said, 'Strip.'

He told her, 'I do *not* turn invisible.'

She said, 'No, but you sure turn red. Don't worry, we're just going for a swim.'

Two minutes later, four bewitching and giggling young women appeared on the patio – wearing, for all practical purposes, nothing. A dozen or so late hangers-on sat at poolside tables, talking quietly and sipping drinks. Heads turned and lounge chairs creaked in acknowledgment of the new quality added to nighttime bathing, and a middle-aged man sitting alone stood up to get a better view.

Two of the girls mounted the diving platform and went into a wild go-go routine under the floodlight there, while the other two gyrated at the water's edge just below.

A uniformed deputy sheriff moved into view across the way, arms crossed and head tilted to the diving platform.

And no one noticed the tall, lithe man in jockey shorts who strode from the shadows of a bungalow, quickly crossed the few yards of flagstones, and quietly entered the waters of the pool. None noticed, that is except the four young women. They joined him then, diving in with playful shrieks and clustering about him in the water.

At the same moment, another man ran panting and wild-eyed into the main lobby to tell a breathless story of murder and kidnapping.

Bolan had swum away from the cops once, but that had been at Miami Beach and in the Atlantic Ocean. Now he was wondering if he could do as well treading water in a hotel pool at Vegas, with four dutiful attendants to keep reminding him how sweet life could be.

He felt a soft body gently gyrating against his beneath the water and a warm voice with a barely noticeable French accent was telling him, 'You are a very attractive man, to be a killer.'

For some odd reason, Bolan at that moment thought of Carl Lyons and of something the cop had said to him during that soft run into town such a short while earlier.

The busty blonde was hanging on to his shoulder and playfully touseling his hair. 'Some killer,' she said. 'He didn't even bring his gun.'

The breathless French accent protested, 'Oh, but I think he has a very nice gun.'

'Oh well,' Bolan said to no one in particular, 'we do our best . . .'

CHAPTER SEVEN

BIG WINNER

VITO APOSTINNI was a highly cautious *Mafioso*, and a cunning one. He had to be, to survive in a job which called for a continual and ever-changing mixture of vigilance, diplomacy, instinctive know-how, and ruthlessness. Casino bosses are not generally renowned for longevity on the job, especially not in the mob casinos – and the Gold Duster was one of the oldest and largest mob joints on the strip. One had to be always certain to whom one was speaking, especially in the delicate matter of okaying credit and other rare privileges. One might even be speaking to an absentee and off-the-record owner, or to a close friend or associate of the same – or one could even be dealing with a fallen-from-grace ex-friend and *persona non gratá*, a 'leper', in the constantly shifting and treacherous jungle of the underworld social register.

Vito Apostinni, in sixteen years on the job, had never once crossed the wrong guy nor had he ever been 'taken' by a smooth operator. That sort of record spelled success for a casino operator – if he could keep his other business in order, as well. For instance, a successful boss had better keep his winning percentages in good shape. Any continuing decline or bad run could begin to look suspicious. He should not drink too much, become overtly ostentatious in his personal habits, nor indulge in too much action at his own tables. He also had better pay close attention to his skim percentages and accomplish the regular rake-offs without getting caught by state gaming agents or by the ever-present Internal Revenue boys.

This latter consideration was most important. The skim off the top, much of it, was used to settle off-the-record interests of owners who could not be issued casino licenses due to a narrow-minded state law which forbade the licensing of persons with criminal records. The Gold Duster was carrying more than a dozen such undercover partners, each of whom was provided weekly accountings and off-the-top payoffs. They got their regular profits too, of course – through their fronts – along with the other stockholders at dividend time, but there was always a need for black money in the lucrative cash markets of the underworld. The casinos provided an ever-flowing river of cash – hard cash – for quick opportunities and even larger profits in those market places.

Skim was also routinely funnelled into the 'grease' routes, payoffs to various influence peddlers around the country. Much of these undeclared gambling profits also found their way into numbered bank accounts in Panama and Switzerland, for later investments in legitimate enterprises both abroad and at home, through foreign intermediaries.

Vito was a consummate skim artist. He had worked out a detection-proof system which would make a stage magician sick with envy. Vito's system was no ordinary sleight-of-hand routine, however. It was built upon an elaborate code of signals between the dealers, the pit bosses, and the backroom accountants, and it involved a constant juggling of 'fill' and 'draw' records for each table in the casino. A 'fill' constitutes a sum of chips and silver added to a table during a particular shift. A 'draw' is the opposite case, the removal of excess table stakes. Paper currency flows across the game tables, also, from patron to dealer, the patron buying chips from the dealer and the latter immediately depositing the currency through a slot into the lock-box at the bottom of the table. It is this particular bit of action upon which Vito's 'system' is based. Through an elaborate signalling arrangement, a constant tally was kept of the amount of currency going into the lock-boxes, making possible the pre-juggling of balance sheets for the official counts.

The three soberest moments of the day for most professional Vegans are the shift-changes; these are the times for 'the count'. State law demands that a balance sheet for each gaming table be prepared at the end of every shift. All the action stops while the silver and chips are counted, the 'fills' and 'draws' calculated, and the currency from the lock-boxes removed for counting behind locked doors and under extreme security conditions.

For Vito Apostinni, the thrice-daily rituals were the cardinal points of his twenty-four-hour routine. Ordinarily he retired immediately after the 4 a.m. count slept until eleven o'clock, had breakfast, a shower, a shave, and a rubdown – in that order – and he was back on hand again for the noon count. Afternoons were a time for relaxation, for visiting with old friends and cultivating new ones, for 'juicing' visiting politicos and other important transients, and for attending to image-making community functions.

Five o'clock to seven were his 'paperwork hours,' during which time he studiously reviewed shifts audits, pit averages, and reports on high rollers and big losers. In gambling parlance, a high roller is a person who consistently bets heavily at the tables.

At seven o'clock Apostinni had his second and final meal of the day, usually a twenty-four-ounce steak, a dry roll, and a half head of lettuce without dressing. He always dined alone, usually in seclusion, and all of his food was prepared by the same chef, a man of unquestioned loyalty who had been with Vito for sixteen years.

At eight o'clock he presided over the final count of the day and began his own official workday, remaining on the casino floor and personally supervising the action until the 4 a.m. count. Vito was the hardest working boss on the strip – or anywhere in the valley for that matter – and he was generally acknowledged as such. The forty-eight-year-old bachelor maintained his only residence on the premises in a specially-constructed efficiency apartment above the casino, and he literally lived on the job – rarely going into the adjacent hotel except to pay respects to a visiting dignitary or to use the eighteen-hole pro golf course. He was soft-spoken, articulate, apparently well educated, and he was generally respected by his employees.

With a strong instinct for image-making, a week never passed when Vito did not appear at some civic function, always with a staff-publicist in the close background taking notes and pictures. He was 'generous' in his regular donations to local churches and community service organizations, and at least once every day he 'came across' for a heavy loser who had gone broke at the Gold Duster, providing the victim with a non-negotiable airline ticket and a hundred dollars in cash, deliverable at the airport boarding gate by a staff publicist with camera. Of such frail and insignificant charities was fostered the image of 'Heart of Gold Vito', a romantic reincarnation of the old Mississippi gambling men who would never let a victim slink away stone broke.

The publicists were never around at count time, when the take was being martialed and massaged into tidy balance sheets of fraud, theft, and conspiracy. And even after the massage, the Gold Duster's official gross profits still managed to hover in the $20,000,000 per year bracket.

Publicity pictures were also not taken of those rare instances when a dealer was discovered working his own personal brand of fraud and theft, and the ensuing grim moments in the back room where 'security agents' pulverized the culprit's hands with steel bars or emblazoned large X's on the backs of the thieving hands with a red-hot branding iron.

One could always count on the photographers, however, when a 'system freak' or high roller cashed in big at the tables, and the pictures usually found their way into the wire press services for nationwide consumption in addition to receiving full ballyhoo along the Strip. And if the big winner did not have sense enough to immediately flee with his winnings, he would find himself hurriedly ensconced in the Gold Duster's 'Winner's Suite' – a luxurious pad with instant service, revolving bed partners, and every enticement imaginable to assure his reappearance on the casino floor. And the picture-taking did not end there; it was just beginning. A battery of television 'eyes' were concealed in the Winner's Suite, recording every breath the unsuspecting sucker took – and also every bed partner. Seldom did a 'big winner' – once the ballyhoo was ended – manage to get out of town with even the stake that had brought him there.

Yes, 'Heart of Gold' Vito was the hardest working casino boss on the Strip – and this particular day had been the most trying accumulation of experiences in Vito's memory. First, it had been that Autry character, posing as a high roller and all the time nosing around in the Gold Duster's entertainment department and trying to rumble the showgirls. Then that damn spot-audit team from Carson City peering over everybody's shoulders during the eight o'clock count. Then the heist of Vito's $60,000 share of the finance shipment and the shaking news from Joe the Monster that Bastard Bolan was behind it. And then the Autry guy turning up missing, and Joe's minions turning the Strip upside down – and then, to end it all, the word that the Taliferos were swooping in with their army of torpedoes.

A war with Bolan this town could definitely do without. It was bad for business. Vito could not understand the Eastern Gentlemen allowing this sort of thing to go on in the open city. The flow of blood would most certainly dry up the flow of money – nervous visitors would be scared away by the sounds of battle – and wasn't that the whole idea behind declaring Vegas an open territory? Wasn't it to keep the trouble down, to keep the image intact, and to keep the bucks flowing in?

Vito just couldn't understand it. If Bolan wanted to pick up a few bucks, wanted to pull a little skim job of his own – then hell, why not let him? Let him take it and get the hell out – that little bit of skim was chickenfeed and meant nothing at all in comparison with the overall losses a shooting war would inevitably mean. Vegas did not need to be 'buttoned down'. Vegas survived and thrived only because there were no buttons. A town that pulled in $400–$500 million a year certainly deserved something better than a vendetta war by the men hired to *protect* the interests there. *Holy Mother.* Vito Apostinni didn't understand any of it.

And already it was too late to do anything about it. The action had moved from Hard Mountain to Paradise Valley, and Paradise was already tasting the flow of blood. And it was Apostinni blood that was being tasted, that was the hardest part.

Vito had not meant that Joe Fuge and Harry Stanners go over there and get themselves into a shooting. They were security agents, not hardmen, bonded and credentialed by the casino owner's association, strictly legitimate in every way and authorized for unrestricted access to any casino on the strip. Vito had not sent them over there to get into a gunfight. Vegas was no place for that kind of action. The idea had been to talk some sense into that Anders fink, and to find out just where the hell he stood with this other troublemaker, this Autry guy. It had seemed a sensible thing to do, especially with Autry on the loose and maybe even a federal spy.

So they'd run into Bolan instead and *what* a mess. Well . . . nobody could blame Vito Apostinni for the mess. His only hope now was that the thing could be handled quietly from here on out, that Bolan could be grabbed and hustled off somewhere out of sight and out of mind before he began affecting business.

And, in the meantime, business had to go on as best it could. It was that cardinal point of the day again, time for the four o'clock count – the biggest and most important of the day – and to hell with Mack the Bastard Bolan and his fancy-Dan damn fireworks.

Apostinni was in the counting room, and his heart of gold was running over with the impressive tabulations being posted. A crew of female tellers were working their way through bales of folding money and the coin counting machines were clicking hungrily under the flood of coins from the slots.

'Looks like the best night this month, Mr. Apostinni,' the head accountant predicted.

'Yeah, well – tell me that again after you've run your slips,' the boss said pleasantly. 'Don't gloat over grosses, you wait and show me what we took.' But Vito was already gloating himself. He knew the house averages, the mathematics of chance, and he did not need an accountant to tell him that it had been a good night.

'I'm going to bed,' he announced tiredly. 'Send the slips up, I'll go over them at breakfast.'

Vito went to the door and waited patiently while the guard worked the combination. He exited into a short hallway and again had to wait while another guard worked the intricacies of the buffer door which admitted him to the casino floor.

His tagman, Max Keno, was awaiting him just outside, boredly watching the action at a blackjack table to while away the time. Apostinni passed on through, smiling affably at familiar faces, the tagman following a discreet few paces behind. Then he spotted Joe the Monster Stanno bearing down on him from the other side of the casino; Vito's smile dwindled away as he halted beside a roulette wheel and awaited the harbinger of trouble.

The huge triggerman pulled up beside him and spoke from the corner of his mouth. 'Morning, Mr. Apostinni. How's it going?'

'Great I guess,' Vito told him. 'How's your end?'

'Rotten. Those dumb cops had that guy sewed up down there and then let 'im get away clean.'

'Too bad,' Apostinni commented unemotionally.

'Yeh. We're still wondering how he did it. Left his car behind. Don't worry, we're watching it.'

'Maybe he's laying low, right there in the place. It's a big place, more'n three hundred rooms.'

'Nah. We tore that joint apart, room by room. He ain't there. But don't you worry. He won't show his face on the Strip again tonight, bet on that.'

'You got things pretty well covered, have you Joe?'

'Double covered. I got the entire Strip security bunch looking out for him. Also everybody else that draws a salary in this valley. Don't you worry, Mr. Apostinni.'

'Okay I won't. I'm tired, Joe, and I'm going to bed. When, uh, when are your bosses due in?'

'About six. They're coming in the company plane. You can feel secure, Mr. Apostinni.'

'I do, Joe. Thanks.'

Vito went on then, the faithful tagman right behind, and the two of them climbed the private stairway to his soundproofed apartment above the casino.

The bodyguard sighed and dropped into a chair at the top of the stairs. Vito continued on to the ornate door, depressed an intercom button, and announced, 'It's Vito, Bruce. It's also 4.22 and all is well.'

The coded announcement would assure the bodyguard-doorkeeper inside that the boss was coming in alone and of his own will. The slightest variation, of words or even tonal quality, would mean sudden death for anyone else trying to crash the apartment with or without the boss.

A buzzer sounded and the door clicked open. Apostinni stepped quickly inside and pushed the door closed. A pencil-flood was spotting him from a raised platform built along the wall, several yards down from the doorway, the shadowy bulk of a man fuzzily outlined behind the light.

Vito faced into the light for a long moment, then irritably said, 'It's just me, Bruce. Cut the damn light.'

'He can't Vito,' advised an icy voice behind him.

Cold steel touched the nape of the casino boss' neck and

the no-nonsense voice told him, 'If you're packing hardware, now's the time to use it or lose it.'

'I'm not packing,' Apostinni replied hastily, his throat suddenly dry and scratchy. What, he wondered, the hell was Bruce doing?

'Don't even breathe hard,' the voice suggested.

Vito did not. He felt, rather than heard or saw, the man moving past him – then the pencil-flood went off and the soft, indirect lighting along the walls came up and Vito got his first good look at the guy the whole organization was screaming about.

Yeah. Bolan the Bastard. A big guy, standing somewhere above six feet high, dressed all in black in a skintight whattayacallit – commando suit or something – black sneakers on his feet. An ammo belt was slung at his waist, and this also supported a flap-type army holster on his right hip, with probably a .45 inside.

Another harness crossed his chest to put a snap-out rig beneath his left arm. The rig was empty now, and a mean looking black blaster with a silencer was filling the guy's big fist.

That face had been carved out of hot steel and freeze-dried, and looking into those goddamn eyes was worse than looking into the bore of the blaster. Vito's eyes flinched away from the confrontation and up the security tower to find Bruce, or the remains of Bruce. The area between the bodyguard's eyes was missing. One eye was laying out on the cheek, blood all over the goddamn place, and Bruce was just sitting there, the body sagging into the seat harness.

Vito's stomach lurched and his eyes fled that place, also. 'H-how'd you get in here dressed like that?' he asked in a choked voice.

'Is that the *last* thing you want to know, Vito?' the cold voice inquired.

'No, forget it, I don't care. What do you want, money? Hell, it's yours, take it, take all of it.'

'Money means nothing to me, Vito,' that voice said.

What kind of a guy did money mean nothing to? Heart of Gold Vito could not understand a guy like that. He said, 'Look, Bolan, I'm clean. I'm a good man, I live a clean life. I do my job and I do it good, and I spread my money around, I mean I give to the poor and needy, you know? Why d'you want to come busting in here, scaring me this way? You got no beef with me.'

The guy grabbed him and shoved him across the room, the blaster tracking him all the way. Vito stumbled to a couch and sat down, his legs no longer willing to support his weight. He whimpered, 'Okay, I'll level, I'm just fronting the joint. I'm a hired hand, I work for a salary, I practically punch a time clock. I'm small, Bolan, small fish. I got no say in anything, I just do what I'm told.'

'Prove it,' the bastard said, in that same cold economy of words.

'All right, so I got an interest too, myself. But it's a small one.'

The guy just stared at him.

'Okay, I can prove it. Let me open the safe. I'll show you black and white.'

The voice behind him again warned, 'Carefully, Vito. Anything goes wrong, Vito, you're the first to get it.'

'Don't worry, I know that,' Apostinni said. He moved jerkily across the room and swung a hinged chest away from the wall, deactivated an electronic alarm system, and opened the safe.

The voice behind him warned, 'Carefully, Vito.'

With extreme care and in almost comic slow motion, the casino boss reached into the small safe and brought out a leather-covered notebook – the most carefully guarded possession of a lifetime. It didn't matter, he kept telling himself. The guy would never get out of here with it alive anyhow, and it might just save Vito's cautious life.

He carefully placed the notebook on the chest and stepped back a respectful distance. 'Just take a look,' he urged. 'That's the whole setup in there, the weekly payoffs, how much and who to. That's the book, Bolan, the *real* book.'

The guy flipped through the pages, grunted, then tucked the notebook into his belt. 'Not enough, Vito,' he said coldly. 'Tell me something interesting that could keep you living a while longer.'

Apostinni's legs gave way again, the thing was clearly way out of hand now. He wobbled to a chair and slumped into it. 'Like what?' he asked miserably.

'I don't know. It's your joint. Entertain me, Vito.'

'I, uh . . .' Apostinni licked his lips and swung his head from side to side as though looking for a miracle. None was in evidence. What did the bastard want? He didn't want money. He didn't want the book. But he hadn't killed Vito *yet*, so what . . .? 'I, uh, you've got the pat hand, Bolan. For now. But listen, you're in a bad spot, you've gotta know that. You better cut out of this town. Joe Stanno and all his boys are turning the whole valley upside down. And the sherriff's boys, they're shaking the town too.'

'Yeah, I know,' the cold bastard told him. He just stood there, staring, that black blaster never wavering an inch away from that spot directly between Vito's eyes.

'Well maybe this is something you don't know,' the desperate man choked out. 'Pat and Mike are due in town in about an hour. They're coming after your head, *paisano*, and those boys don't fool around. They're bringing a jet plane full of soldiers with them, and they're the hardest soldiers in the business. I guess you know that.'

'Yeah,' the guy said, unimpressed.

'Bolan . . . I got three hundred and seventy-five grand in the vault downstairs. Think of that. Say the word and it's yours. Every cent, I swear, it's all yours.'

'What would I do with all that money, Vito?'

'Hell I – buy yourself a pardon. I know a hundred guys could grease the slide for you. Hell I bet I could do it myself, I know lots of people, everybody, important people. Let me—'

'Shut up, Vito.'

'For God's sake, Bolan, why d'you want to kill *me*?'

Vito was starting to sweat, 'I'm a nobody, a nickel and dime front man. I'm not even worth the price of your bullet. Why *me*?'

'I'm trying to think of a reason why *not*, Vito.'

'Well *God*, I can give you plenty of reasons why not.'

'Look at it from my point of view, Vito. Then just give me one.'

'Well I – okay. Okay. I can get you out of here in one piece, Bolan. Joe Stanno is downstairs right now. There's no way out of here except past Joe Stanno. Joe the Monster, you've heard of him I know. I can guarantee you safe passage, Bolan.'

'I got myself in,' the rotten bastard replied. 'I'll get myself back out.'

'Okay! Wait a minute Bolan! For God's sake – okay, listen! What do you want? Something hot? Something really big?'

'You're getting close, Vito.'

'Well I . . .' Apostinni sent his gaze in a dazed search of his surroundings, as though wondering if it were really happening. He'd had this rooftop addition put on here like an oversized vault, just to keep nuts like this *out*. Now here was one *in*, and Heart of Gold Vito was *in* with him, and God there wasn't *no* way out. The odds of anybody coming up to look in on him, at this hour, were about a million to one. Everybody knew this was Vito's bedtime, nobody would come up disturbing him now.

Vito did not want to die like this, not this way, locked up with a lunatic gunsel who'd rather kill than be rich. If he could just talk the guy along . . . give him something, hell anything, and hope and pray for a break. Holy Mother, just one break. What a hell of a cold deck for Vito.

'What'd you say, Vito?' the icy bastard asked him.

'I said . . . if you want something big, I mean really *big* . . . how about the carousel? You on to that yet?'

Something flickered there in the big guy's eyes, an interest maybe. Apostinni plunged on hopefully. 'Yeah, that's the big one coming up. The Caribbean carousel, I'll bet you've heard a rumble or two on that.'

'Back up and try it again,' Bolan said, the blaster still centered between Vito's eyes.

'Try what?'

'What kind of carousel?'

'You know, a merry-go-round, that kind of carousel.'

The big guy's eyes got speculative, and he said, 'Something like the California carousel, eh?'

'Nah, that's just the L.A. end, that's nothing. The Caribbean is where it's all at now, Bolan, that's the next big one.'

'Okay. Keep trying.'

'Hell, that's all I know right now. They don't let small fish like me in on details like that. But I've personally dispatched sixteen mil down there in the past year.'

'Sixteen million dollars?'

'That's it. And that boodle you heisted out there tonight was headed for the same place.'

'The Caribbean, eh.'

The guy was interested. Apostinni's heart got a bit stronger and he said, 'Yeh. San Juan first. There it's cut and sent around the carousel to the other islands.'

'For what?'

'I don't know for what. I'm leveling with you, Bolan.'

'Suppose I give you a reprieve, Vito. For twenty-four hours. Think you could come up with something a bit more worthwhile?'

'Sure, I know I could.'

'You're small fish, remember?'

'To live, Bolan, I can get big damn quick.'

'Okay, you've bought yourself a day, Vito. Honor the deal and I'll make it a full pardon.'

Apostinni could hardly believe it. The guy couldn't be that stupid! 'God, you can trust me, Bolan. I never welched a deal in my life.'

'Okay.'

The guy just stood there, staring at him from behind the blaster. Apostinni coughed nervously and said, 'Well ... okay. I'll uh, escort you out. Meet me back here tomorrow, same time. Or would you rather I meet you some place?'

'Right here will be fine.'

The guy just *stood* there. The boss of the Gold Duster got to his feet and crossed carefully to the door. Was the hick dum-rube bastard going to let him actually walk out of there?

Vito carefully placed his hand on the door mechanism and, with every nerve of his body screaming for control, told Bolan, 'You want me to go on ahead and, uh, clear a path for you?'

'Okay,' said the jerk-probably hophead, unbelievably stupid dummy.

Apostinni opened the door, slid out, banged it shut, hit the panic switch and froze that door so a ton of TNT wouldn't open it and started alarms ringing all over the joint, and all in the same instant he screeched, 'Max! That nut's in there! What the goddamn hell're you—'

The tagman was out of his chair and lunging toward the boss, the rod in his hand, trying to surround his personal god with his own lone body.

'Wait, waitaminnit!' Vito cried, shoving the bodyguard away from him. 'He's locked in *there*, dammit!'

The casino boss punched the intercom button and yelled, 'Okay, dummy, that's all for you. That's a regular vault you're in there, you dumb shit!'

A wave of humanity was surging up the stairway, pistols waving all over the place, and towards the rear of the wave Joe the Monster was pushing people this way and that and fighting his way to the front.

'What the hell is it, Vito?' Stanno yelled.

'That nut, that Bolan dummy, I got 'im locked up inside my joint!' Apostinni cried exultantly.

'Well shut off the fuckin' alarms, huh?'

A full sixty seconds were required to still the pandemonium outside 'Vito's joint' and to line up a wavy wedge of gun soldiers, and then another twenty seconds to override the electric lock. Then the door was flung open and six of Joe the Monster's best dived through the opening, guns blazing in every direction.

It took less than three seconds to completely shoot up Vito's joint.

And when the firing ended, Joe the Monster stepped warily into the room, gazed stupidly around at his boys, and then called out, 'Mr. Apostinni. Who'd you say was locked up in here?'

'Didn't you get him?' Vito asked in a hushed voice.

Another voice sang out from inside. 'Nobody in the bathroom, Joe.'

Apostinni entered the 'vault' on trembling legs. 'He *couldn't* have got out,' he insisted in a dazed voice.

'Who shot Bruce Serena, Mr. Apostinni?' Stanno swiveled about to glare at his guncrew. 'Did one of your boys drill Bruce Baby?'

'*They* didn't do it!' Apostinni cried. 'That Bolan bastard did it, and he was going to do it to me too! I outsmarted him and made a break! Look, dammit, he's *in* here *some*where!'

'Should we look under the rug, Mr. Apostinni? We looked every place else.'

'I'm telling you he's in here!' the casino boss ranted. 'There ain't no way out! He's *in* here!'

'Mr. Apostinni,' Joe the Monster said quietly, 'you been working just a little too hard. You better get to bed now. Get some sleep. I'll handle the explanations downstairs.'

'I'm telling you he's *in* here! I ain't sleepin' in here until you *find* him!'

'Somebody pull Bruce Baby down from there,' Stanno commanded, sighing. 'Where's the gun, Mr. Apostinni? You better let me get rid of it.' Stanno signaled to Max

Keno, the surviving bodyguard. 'Come on now, Mr. Apostinni, we got to take care of ourselves, right?'

'Look, Joe, I'm not off my marbles.' Vito declared, his voice now cold and controlled. 'I didn't drill Bruce, I'm telling you—'

'Hey boss!' cried an excited voice from the security platform. Two hardmen had gone up to bring Bruce Baby down. Now one of them was leaning forward with something in his hand. 'This was in his lap.'

Stanno and Apostinni hurried over to the tower and the hardman dropped his find into the enforcer's outstretched hand. It was a sheet of note paper, with something heavier folded inside. A marksman's medal slid out of the fold.

Stanno cleared his throat, which had suddenly become very tight, and read aloud the message that was printed neatly on the paper. The message was, simply, 'Twenty-four hours, Vito.'

'See, I told you,' Apostinni murmured in a voice with everything suddenly gone out of it.

With cold frustration, Stanno growled, 'Well, how the hell did he . . .?'

The men on the tower were intensely occupied with another find. 'What's this up here on the wall?' one cried. 'Boss! This thing is loose! It's . . .'

'What is it?' Stanno yelled.

Apostinni died a little further and mumbled, 'The accessory shaft.'

'The what?'

'You know,' Goldhearted Vito whispered. 'Air conditioning, power cables, TV lead-in, all that.'

'Well where does it go to?' Joe the Monster fumed.

'Out back I guess, Joe.'

'You *guess*?' Stanno clapped his hands together and dispatched a gun party to check it out. The hardmen bolted away and Stanno yelled at the men on the tower: 'Well go on, go on through!'

But it was too late, Apostinni knew in his heart, for a hot pursuit now. The casino boss had been high-rolled by a real pro, and he was experiencing a new and terrifying insight into the mathematics of chance.

The guy had just casually dropped in, allowed Vito to hand over his black book, and then just dropped the hell back out again.

Some men *made* their chances, others merely rode with them.

And Heart of Gold Vito would never again be absolutely certain as to which category he himself fit into.

CHAPTER EIGHT

COMBAT BRIEF

A NEGRO beauty in a nurse's uniform opened the door to Bolan's third buzz. Her eyes recoiled somewhat as the black-clad figure stepped inside the private clinic, then she giggled and told him, 'I didn't know you in your soul underwear.'

'How's the patient?' Bolan asked her.

'Doing fine,' the nurse reported, lowering her voice to a whisper. 'Doctor looked in on him at four o'clock. He's going to be all right.'

'Is he sedated?'

She shook her head. 'No, he's resting easily.'

'It's very important that I talk to him, Mrs. Thomas.'

The woman pursed her lips as she studied Bolan's face, then she smiled and told him, 'Just a sec. I'll ask Doctor.'

Bolan watched her disappear through a doorway off the lobby, and again he reflected upon Lyons' determination to remain in his role. The clinic was situated in the city's Westside, in the Negro district. There was a personal relationship of some sort between Lyons and the doctor, and the cop had insisted upon being brought here. The setup seemed ideal to Bolan, and apparently Lyons was in the best of hands. Still . . . Bolan had an uneasiness about the thing.

A tired looking black man appeared in the doorway, wearing pajamas and a cotton robe. He looked Bolan up and down, then wryly commented. 'I see you're dressed for destruction. Why do you want to talk to Carl?'

'It's urgent,' Bolan assured him.

'He's resting good. Can't it wait at least until daylight?'

'It can. But maybe I can't.'

The doctor understood. He stared at the visitor through a brief silence, then he jerked his head and said, 'Okay. Don't take too long.'

Bolan said, 'Sure,' and went on along the corridor and into Lyons' room. The doctor's wife had gotten there ahead of him and she was quietly rousing the ailing cop.

'You have a visitor, Carl,' he heard her say.

A dim lamp on a side table had the room in soft shadows. The cop was flat on his back, no pillows. His left arm was tied to the bed and he was getting an intravenous drip-injection from a bottle of clear fluid in a bedside stand.

Bolan moved in on the other side. Lyons looked him over and said, 'You're blitzing.'

'Softly,' Bolan replied.

The nurse cautioned, 'Don't get him too excited,' and she made a quiet exit.

'What's up?' the cop asked.

'Maybe a hell of a lot. First, though, I brought you a gift.'

Bolan produced Vito Apostinni's black book and placed it in Lyons' free hand. 'Don't try to look at it now. It's the black money ledger on the Gold Duster operation.'

'How the hell did you get that?' Lyons asked with a grin.

'I traded Vito his life for it.'

The cop's grin faded. 'Some trade.'

'Yeah. Uh, your funny man is okay. For now. He told me about ASA and the show biz muscle.'

Lyons smiled and commented, 'It's hard to keep a secret in this town.'

'But that's not the all of it, is it? It goes a lot bigger than Anders, doesn't it?'

Lyons gave him an odd look and replied, 'I can't talk about that, Mack. New subject, please.'

Bolan said, 'New subject, hell. My game is survival, remember? I need everything I can possibly use.'

'There's a place where friendship ends,' the cop muttered stubbornly.

A smile formed at Bolan's lips and stayed there, unable to influence the eyes. A cop's ethics could be a curious thing, he was thinking. A cop like Lyons would bust his own mother for pandering, then promise her immunity from prosecution if she'd turn state's evidence against her pimp. It was a game called 'law enforcement' – a very close cousin to the game of survival – and Bolan could understand games like these.

'I didn't come begging,' he said. 'I came trading. I gave you Vito's book. Now what the hell am I getting in return?'

The cop sighed. The grin returned. 'Not much,' he promised.

'California carousel,' Bolan said, getting right to the heart. 'I figured it was an operational code. It's not. So what is it?'

'It's a mob circuit. One big wheel, turning endlessly.'

'Turning what?'

'Everything. Talent, sex, narcotics, contraband, black money, extortion, corpses. You name it, the carousel's turning it.'

'How does L.A. get into the action? I mean, what's your interest?'

'We have a seaport, remember? Also the major international airport in the west. And we have a border with a foreign country. Do I have to lay it all out?'

'So what's new?' Bolan asked. 'That's been going on since year one.'

The cop sighed. 'What's new is the combination.'

After a moment of silence, Bolan said, 'Okay, I'm listening.'

'You can quit listening. This is where you go to hell, buddy.'

Bolan whistled softly. 'That big, eh? *Top Secret* and all that?'

'Something like that,' Lyons growled.

'Okay, just clue me. Then I'll drop something on you that's maybe bigger.'

The cop's eyes were speculative, wary. Quietly, he said, 'Get out of here, Mack.'

'I actually do have something.'

Lyons let his breath all the way out and sighed, 'Okay. Vegas is where the brass ring is at. That help you any?'

'Sure. But I still want to know about that combination.'

'You tell me something interesting first,' Lyons suggested.

'The eye of the brass ring in Vegas is the Gold Duster,' Bolan said quietly.

'Do tell. Why d'you think I broke my body there?'

'But it's like the eyepiece of a telescope. Another ring is at the other end, much larger, a hell of a lot more important.'

Lyons was interested. 'And what is that?' he asked.

Bolan smiled. 'What's that new combination?'

The cop smiled back and muttered, 'Bastard.'

'Are we playing or not?'

'Red China,' Lyons said.

'What?'

'Yeah. How's that for a mob combination? And the trade, we hear, is lively.'

'In what?'

'In everything. It's developing into the largest invisible market in the world.'

Bolan said, 'Well it figures.'

'What figures?'

'That other brass ring. It's within shouting distance of Havana.'

The cop's eyes flashed. 'Miami?'

Bolan shook his head. 'Not the way I hear it, but Miami is probably somewhere in the loop. My information says that San Juan is the eye of the needle. They're calling it the Caribbean carousel.'

Lyons chewed the news for a moment, then asked, 'How good *is* your information?'

'Practically a dying confession,' Bolan told him. 'Straight from the scared-out-of-his-skull lips of Vito Apostinni.'

'A guy will say anything at a time like that, Mack.'

'Not that guy. He thought I was a dead man, too, and it was quite a poker game. No . . . I think he was leveling.'

'It makes sense,' the cop admitted. He sighed and said, 'Bye bye, Bolan. The fuzz is getting fuzzy-headed.'

'One more thing. It's a long route from Peking to Tommy Anders. What's the angle there?'

The cop's voice was weary in the reply. 'That was our best route of entry, and I drew the short straw. Anders *is* in big trouble – and I've been worried about him. I mean, he's an okay guy – lots of guts – and I'd hate to see him a casualty of this mess. I mean . . .'

'You mean you've been using him.' Bolan said. 'And now it's hurting.'

Lyons shrugged with his eyebrows. 'Name of the game,' he replied. 'That isn't the whole thing, Mack. It's a rotten picture all the way, and the show business angle is as scary as any. The mob is clawing their way into Hollywood even. If the movie industry think they're in trouble now, just wait until the *mob* starts gangbanging 'em.'

'How does that fit into the carousel thing?'

Lyons frowned and said, 'Hell, how doesn't it figure? Movies are big business. Distributing and exhibiting the finished product is even bigger. Once the mob has control in that arena they've got the most beautiful damn carousel you ever saw – for any damn kind of game they choose to play. Anything from popcorn concessions to theatre equipment, box office skim, and commercial dates with the starlets.'

'What kind of claws are they using?' Bolan wondered aloud.

'The best kind there is. Money. When money is tight, *black* money is king. The guy that controls the purse also runs the show. In any business.'

'But it all fits together somewhere, doesn't it? On the merry-go-round, I mean.'

'Sure,' Lyons said. 'You know how the mob operates. They carve all the action into private concessions. One family has the entertainment concession. Another specializes in the narcotics angle. Still another gets the contraband. And on and on endlessly – a carousel, yeah. Now you're saying Havana, eh? Hell, that could mean anything. From atomic secrets to small revolutions to a whorehouse in Guantanamo Bay.'

'Or . . .' Bolan suggested quietly, 'a new Vegas.'

'Yeah, that's possible. There's a lot of action in the Caribbean already.'

'And the heat in this town is getting pretty fierce, isn't it? For the mob, I mean. How many dealers and shills and coin-girls do you figure are on the FBI payroll?'

Lyons snickered. 'You noticed.'

'Sure I noticed. And don't think the boys haven't noticed. When the heat gets too high, Lyons, the mob moves on. If they can't fight it or buy it, they leave it. Vito let it drop that he sent sixteen million to San Juan in one year. And that's just from one casino.'

Musingly, the cop said, 'Even our esteemed local billionaire has shaken the dust of Vegas from his feet . . . and moved on to . . .'

Bolan's eyebrows formed a peak. 'I've never heard anything tying him to—'

'No I wasn't saying that,' Lyons replied. 'But you don't make a billion by playing the losers. Maybe he knows something the rest of us don't.'

'Like, maybe Vegas is dying.'

'Like maybe something like that,' Lyons said, sighing.

'Bug off, will you? I can't keep my eyes open another minute. You heard the nurse, don't excite me.'

Bolan grinned and said, 'Okay. You lay here and snooze while I go play cop.'

'Take a friend's advice and stay out of it, Mack. The feds are waltzing this thing along with a very delicate touch. I told you what Brognola said. That will go double, here in Vegas. They'll take no interference, buddy.'

'I'm not competing with the feds,' Bolan replied. 'But I'm not playing tiddley-winks, either, and I need every handle I can get. I'm going to bust this town, Lyons.'

'Don't. You've done enough already. Just pick up your chips and get out while you can.'

'Too late for that now,' Bolan told his friend. 'From what I overheard on Vito's pipeline, my only chance is a sweep through the middle.' He grinned. 'Did you know, that guy's got his own casino bugged, ears everywhere.'

Lyons smiled faintly. 'In this town, nobody trusts anybody. And, I've learned, with damn good reason.'

'Well, I'm going to flavor their pots a bit.'

'Some Bolan spice, eh?'

'Something like that.'

'Be careful, dammit,' the cop said fiercely.

'My heart even beats careful,' Bolan told him, and that was his parting line.

He went back along the corridor, thanked the nurse, and re-invaded the night. There was not much of it left – it was nearly dawn and almost time for the next maneuver.

The Executioner had a plane to meet.

CHAPTER NINE

A DASH OF BOLAN

Bolan was not only an expert marksman, he was also a highly skilled armorer – or gunsmith, to use the civilian term. His expertise with destructive weapons extended into areas of military ordnance, munitions and various types of explosive devices. He was a weapons specialist and his warwagon reflected this facet of the Bolan threat. It was a rolling arsenal, featuring the most advanced and versatile selection of arms available in the secret market-places.

Of all the weapons in the collection, however, his most cherished possession was a non-military piece, a sports-man's big-game rifle which could be purchased almost anywhere – though this particular one had been highly refined and 'worked-in' – a Weatherby Mark V. He had acquired it during the London adventure, and he'd gone to great trouble and expense to have the weapon for-warded to him upon his return to this country.

The bolt-action piece handled .460 calibre Magnums with a point-blank range of 400 yards, maximum range 1,000 yards, and the big sniperscope that came with it would resolve the head of a pimple a half-mile away. The muzzle energy was 4,000 pounds; the Magnums carried more than 300 grains of push behind the expanding, high-shock projectiles which could tear a man's head off at 500 yards.

The range on the present mission would be much less than that. The only problem Bolan was sweating was the question of light. The scope would be useless in the dark.

If that plane should beat the sun into the target area, Bolan would have to scrub and withdraw. He could not 'work close' on this type of hit. The odds would be too great, the route of retreat too shaky.

There were no doubts regarding the target area. The private jet would almost certainly not use the facilities of the airline terminal, but would taxi to a convenient spot for transferring her passengers directly to waiting automobiles. This was SOP for Mafia war parties. And there had been no problem locating the line-up of crew wagons, the big eight-passenger jobs the mob preferred for their headhunters. The limousines were waiting on a service apron, a hundred yards or so from the flying service building and about two hundred yards from the blast fence which was presently shielding Bolan's van, at the end of the primary runway.

He counted nine vehicles and ran his war party projection from there – sixty to seventy people were arriving. Figure the plane crew at about four, each of them a hardman, from the chief pilot on down. Say then, possibly, seventy-five guns out there, plus the nine wheelmen and maybe a couple of ranking greeters – round it off at even figures and call it ninety guns.

Yeah, those were some odds. Impossible? Scary as hell, sure – but no, not impossible. He would not be trying for a wipe-out . . . a bit of jarring, maybe – spice for the Vegas pot – a pinch of fear and stir well.

And then a new thought occured to him, and a smile played briefly upon the Executioner's face. If the conditions were just right . . . if he could be assured of a clean target and a well-defined safety zone for non-combatants . . . if the sun and the airport traffic would play ball . . . then just maybe he could come up with an alternate target area and an extra pinch for the pot. Yes, and maybe he could show the Talifero brothers just how he felt about their damn warparty.

Part of the Talifero legend was that the brothers had

attended law school at one of the big prestige universities of the east. One story said Yale, another Harvard; still another, probably pure fantasy, claimed that both had attended under a single tuition and alternated at classes.

It was true that the brothers were practically identical in appearance, that they sounded alike, walked alike, and seemed to think alike.

It was also true that they ran a bodyshop to put *Murder, Incorporated* to shame. They enjoyed equal rank with other members of *La Commissione* and their cadre was an elite corps said to be as secretive and effective as the Gestapo of the early Nazis. The Talifero cadre was, in every respect, the invisible secret police force of the organized underworld.

A Taliferi, it was rumored, could hit a *Capo* – without a contract and without fear of reprisal from other bosses. This story could be an exaggeration, but in several instances the brothers had done so, of their own initiative and without prior consultation with the council of bosses. The Taliferi were the most feared and respected force within the Mafia.

One would not receive such an impression, upon a casual encounter with the brothers. They dressed conservatively and impeccably, their speech could be flawless and impressively articulated, their manner urbane, and they smiled a lot – particularly at each other, as though forever sharing some secret joke.

Neither of the brothers was smiling, however, as the big jet began the descent to McCarran Field, just outside Las Vegas. They sat in the forward cabin, the 'business suite', staring stonily out the windows at the gray-dawn landscapes below. Perhaps they were thinking of Miami, and of the terrible time they'd had there with Bolan.

Maybe Pat was thinking of the near-fatal wounds he'd acquired in that meeting. Mike, perhaps, was still smarting over the indignities of being arrested, fingerprinted and booked on a dozen charges by the Dade County police, and of the continuing fight for freedom in a court the clouters just couldn't seem to get a handle on.

Each of the brothers had a lot to be thoughtful about and their thoughts, at such times, inevitably traveled back to the source of all their troubles, that Bolan bastard.

They had sworn the oath of *vendetta*. They must wash their hands in the bastard's blood – and then perhaps they could look at each other without smiling at their secret 'joke' which the bastard had left them with.

The warning lights came on and the pilot's voice came through the PA to announce, 'We're cleared for straight-in. Land in a few minutes.'

The brothers exchanged glances. One of them got to his feet and walked toward the rear to give last minute instructions to 'the boys'. The other stepped into the cockpit and touched the pilot on the shoulder.

'Are they waiting?' he asked.

'Yes sir. No traffic. We're going straight in, runway two-five. I'll just bounce over to the cut-off and wheel right up to the cars.'

'That's fine, Johnny.'

The co-pilot looked up with a grin and asked, 'We going to be here long enough for a little table action, Mr. Talifero?'

'You won't even have time to get laid, Ed,' the boss replied.

Both crewmen chuckled. The pilot asked, 'Figure he'll be that easy?'

'I believe so.' Talifero eased into the jump seat and strapped himself in. 'Unless Joe Stanno ran wild and screwed up everything.'

The pilot grimaced and declared, 'That guy Stanno gives me the shivers. He's a psychopath, you know.'

'A very, *very* valuable one,' Talifero said quietly.

The pilots became very busy then, lining the big craft into the approach lane, adjusting air speed, trim and altitude; threading a precise needle in the air to bring the metal bird to earth. The flaps rumbled into position, the landing gear extended and locked, and the terrain began whizzing past the windows at incredible speed.

Mike Talifero always rode the cockpit during takeoff and landing. It was his way of fighting an unreasonable fear of flying. These were the most dangerous times, or so the experts said, and it was a hell of a lot more frightening up here where the action was. Mike liked to meet fear where it was at – not on any psychiatrist's couch, not praying in a corner somewhere, but right up . . . it was like that with this Bolan deal, he supposed. A man – especially a man like Mike Talifero – had to stand up and meet the action right where it was at.

He was gripping his knees in clenched fists when the wheels touched, squealed, then got in step with the plane's momentum and finally began rolling smoothly along the cement strip. On they rolled, with no noticeable decrease in speed – things flashing by out there in that weird kaleidoscope of objects briefly seen and immediately gone forever.

Then the pilot moved a control and the tons of plunging metal shivered momentarily as the reverse-thrust took hold and the forward momentum began dropping away. Talifero sighed with relief and gripped his safety belt.

'Beautiful, Johnny,' he complimented the pilot, in an entirely composed voice.

And then something went terribly wrong. With the ground speed still holding at above sixty, the plane seemed to wobble and keel toward one side. The co-pilot yelled, 'Starboard blowout!'

The pilot, his face suddenly ashen, was fighting the controls and trying to stabilize the track as the big bird crabbed inexorably into a sideways skid.

The cockpit went into a crazy tilt, a chilling popping and buckling sound groaned up from somewhere below, and the aircraft shuddered and collapsed on to the runway.

And then there was nothing to be heard but the thudding of Mike Talifero's heart and that screeching doomsday sound of the fuselage grinding along on concrete, the kaleidoscope at the windows replaced by a dizzying merry-go-round running out of control.

This was where it was at, man. And out of the peaking chaos of the moment, another certain knowledge shrieked into Talifero's head.

This was also where Bolan was at!

The Executioner had set up his fire base on a small mound of desert earth at the western end of the main runway, positioning himself slightly to one side of the blast fence. He had greeted the arrival of daylight with pleasure, even realizing that in another few minutes the sun would be looming over those distant mountains and that he would be looking directly into it.

In a few minutes, though, the position of the sun in the sky would have no relevance to this mission. He had located his target, verified the identification, and calculated the precise moment of touchdown. The airport was quiet and absolutely devoid of any traffic which might place innocent civilians in jeopardy.

The hands that had rolled destiny's dice had also dealt Bolan a perfect hand for this play at McCarran. The rest would be up to him, and he felt ready for the betting to commence.

The nine wheelmen over by the mob vehicles had unclumped and gone to their cars. A big man whom Bolan could not recognize through his binoculars was arm-waving them around and getting the reception party ready.

And then there was the big bird, swooping in over the approach lighting system and settling on to the far end of the runway.

Bolan lay into the Weatherby and acquired the target in the high-resolution vision field of the scope, then tracked it into the range he wanted. He heard the powerful engines whining into the reverse-thrust as the plane reached the runway intersection, signaling the beginning of the braking action.

A fat rubber wheel rolled into the cross-hairs; Bolan acquired and held, tracking along for a few seconds to get a feel of the rate of closure, then he found his adjustment and sighted into the pull.

The Weatherby roared and bucked and sent an official greeting sizzling toward the war party. He rode the recoil and sent another, then another, before lifting off the eye-piece.

The plane staggered and went into a crab. A wing whipped around and the big bird was sliding sideways momentarily, then the landing gear collapsed and down she went in a pancake on the runway, spinning with a terrible screeching and groaning, and continuing on toward Bolan.

Pandemonium erupted in the vehicle area, the wheel-men leaping from their cars in a frenzy of helpless observation of the staggering event.

The big guy was leaping around and pointing toward Bolan's fire base. Even at this distance it was obvious that he was yelling his head off. Three of the wheelmen began running uncertainly toward Bolan's end of the runway.

He swung the Weatherby into the secondary target area, acquired a darkly frightened face in the crosshairs, and squeezed off. The face abruptly disintegrated and disappeared from the vision field. Bolan looked up from eyepiece to evaluate, and saw that the message had been received and understood. The other two were showing the Executioner their backsides and hastily returning to the security of the group.

The group itself had disappeared, and an ineffectual crackle of handguns was emanating from behind the line of vehicles.

Meanwhile the aircraft was spinning on down the pike and beginning to disintegrate, leaving a trail of debris behind. A wing fell off, then the tail section collapsed and the wreckage spun off the runway settling in a cloud of dust a few hundred feet from Bolan's fire base.

Flames were licking up through a pall of dust and

smoke, and Bolan could hear the shrieks and yells of panicky humanity trying to fight their way clear of the death trap. Then reeling figures began to emerge from the clouded wreckage.

Bolan again leaned into the Weatherby, then changed his mind and lifted off. It was enough, for the moment. The wailing alarms of emergency vehicles were being heard now and Bolan was crowding his time factor. It was okay; they'd gotten the message.

He sent a couple more sizzling rounds into the crew wagons, simply to sound a final discouraging note, then he quickly withdrew.

Welcome to the war – that was the message. A hot welcome – coldly sent, jarringly received.

And, at that very moment, another aircraft was landing at Nellis Air Force Base, just a few miles away. It bore decals of the United States government and it carried a contingent of U.S. marshals and FBI agents. It carried, also, a very grimfaced justice department official and an executive order to end that very war.

The Executioner was crowding his time factor a bit more then he realized.

CHAPTER TEN

THE PROBLEM

GUYS were lying all over the ground. Some were sitting up and feeling around to see if anything was missing, and a few were standing around and dazedly watching the crash trucks trying to smother the fire in the demolished airplane.

Joe Stanno found the Talifero brothers in a quiet consultation with the crash chief. He had a hard time recognizing them and for once they did not look exactly alike. They looked like hell, is what they looked like, and Stanno was surprised that they looked that good.

The monster pushed the crash chief out of the way and growled, 'Go talk to th' pilot, he's laying over there by the ambulance.'

The guy looked at Stanno, started to protest and changed his mind, but stubbornly stayed where he was.

Stanno showed his bosses a woebegone face and told them, 'This is the awfullest thing I ever saw.'

One of the Taliferi, Joe never could tell which, replied, 'It's a miracle that any of us got out alive, Joe.'

The other was dabbing at a congealed cut on his forehead with a handkerchief. He said, 'The chief here was just asking us about gunshots. He says some people here on the ground thought they heard something that sounded like gunshots just before the accident. What did you hear, Joe?'

Stanno took the cue line and replied, 'Yeah, it sounded like gunshots. But it was just those tires blowing.'

'That's what I was just suggesting when you came up.'

The crash chief said, 'The towermen thought they heard shots *after* the crash . . . or during it.'

Stanno growled, 'What the hell does anybody know at a time like that, with so much happening? Just what're you trying to make here?'

The guy replied, 'I'm just trying to ascertain the facts, that's all.'

'*The facts*,' Stanno snarled, 'are that your goddam lousy runway tore up our airplane. Now get outta here!'

The chief calmly replied, 'Well, we'll see,' but he got out of there.

The Taliferi watched the official walk away, then the one with the cut head asked, 'Okay, what's the straight on those shots?'

'Straight as hell, sir,' Stanno replied wearily. 'It was Bolan, with a big rifle. He shot your wheels off.'

Someone sighed loudly and someone else said, 'Well, what about Bolan?'

'I sent some boys down to roust 'im. He cut down Bingy Bigelow on about the third step I guess. The other boys come running back, and I can't blame them. There's no cover out there, and that guy is murder with a big rifle. By this time that airplane is asshole over appetite and that's about all I could think about.'

'How'd the guy know we were coming in?'

'Damned if I know,' Stanno growled.

'He's been in contact with some fink.'

'Well, I – yeah, by God you're right, he's been in contact. I come over here straight from th' Duster. The guy had busted in there and I—'

'What the hell do you mean? He *busted* into our own place?'

'Yessir, he went in there and rumbled Vito and—'

'I somehow find that impossible to understand, Joe.'

'Yessir, me too, and anyway—'

'I told you to fold this town in squarely.'

'Listen, sir, there *ain't* no folding that bastard in

anywhere. I got more than two hundred boys running around this damn town, and that son of a bitch just comes and goes as he pleases. He's been—'

'What was that about Vito?'

'I don't know for sure. I didn't have time to get it all. Had to get this convoy out here to pick you up. Anyway, the guy comes in and talks to Vito. Vito manages to cold-deck him somehow, and the guy leaves.'

Someone made a scoffing sound and someone else said, 'Don't you believe it, Joe. Nobody cold-decks Bolan.'

Stanno said, 'Well, I . . .'

'I guess we should go talk to Vito, eh?' someone said.

Someone else said, 'I can't understand such loose security. There should have been some boys covering this airport, Joe.'

'Well, yessir, there is, but—'

'But not out here on the runways, eh, Joe? Why the hell not?'

Stanno felt the world closing on him. He spat on the ground and flopped one foot out in front of the other and said, 'Christ, who would've figured the asshole to come out here and attack the damn plane, eh?'

Someone said, 'I was under the impression that we were paying somebody to think about things like that.'

Stanno coughed and replied, 'Shit, sir, you don't know what's been going on around here.'

'I don't, eh?' said one of the brothers. 'Who the hell do you think was belly-flopping along the runway in a shot-up airplane? Huh?'

'I was right in there with you, sir,' Stanno replied humbly. 'Honest to Christ, I never felt so terrible about a thing in my life.'

'We flew in here with sixty guns, Joe. We have about forty left, and half of those are bunged up. How many do you figure we'll be able to get into Vegas with?'

'Listen, don't worry,' Joe the Monster growled. 'That bastard won't—'

'You say you have a dead boy on your hands?'

'Yessir. We drug him into one of the cars. Don't worry, we're quieting it about the shooting.'

A guy limped up, ignored Stanno, and addressed the brother with the cut head. 'Okay, I got the walking wounded made,' he reported. 'We got eighteen sheet cases and thirteen stretcher cases. The rest are okay.'

'Get them into the cars over there, Charlie,' the boss ordered. 'Send someone to the hospital to grease for those thirteen boys, I want them to have the best. But first let's get those cars loaded. I want to take off before we get tied down with a lot of damned questions.'

The other brother touched Stanno's arm as the limping man nodded and walked away. He said, 'Don't feel so bad, Joe. You're not the first to be run over by this Bolan.'

'I'm gonna be the *last*,' Stanno promised.

Someone chuckled and someone else said, 'I wonder where I've heard that before.'

That was okay, Joe was thinking. Let the look-alikes snicker. He'd show them who would come up with Bolan's head in a sack.

They weren't so goddamn tough. They were making big noises, yeah. But those brothers were shook, *man* they were shook.

In fact, Joe knew, they were scared outta their goddam gourds.

Harold Brognola stepped into the operations office at Nellis AFB and smilingly accepted the telephone from the duty officer.

'Brognola here,' he announced into the phone. 'Who's this?'

The smile faded and he raised troubled eyes to the duty officer as a crisp voice rattled the telephone receiver.

'He didn't lose much time, did he?' the man from Washington muttered.

Rapidfire speech poured through the receiver. Brognola listened without interruption, his fingers drumming on the operations counter. Then he said, 'Okay, let's not waste any time. We're on our way in – helicopters. Keep someone on their tail and meet me in town . . . say twenty minutes.'

He returned the instrument to the duty officer and asked him, 'Did you get a report on a civil crash at McCarran?'

The officer replied, 'Yes sir. A private jet wiped-out during its landing roll, just a few minutes ago. Gear collapsed or something. The runways are cleared and open, though.'

Brognola thanked the Air Force officer and went back outside. He gave not a damn whether or not the McCarran runways were open. He did give – though – quite a bit of damn about the guy who was undoubtedly behind it all.

He rejoined his party outside the operations office and told the chief marshal, 'That was Bill Miller, FBI district officer. Our friends arrived, okay, but it appears that our eternal warfare expert was on hand at McCarran to welcome them to the city of hope. And from the sound of the report, he disillusioned them right off the bat.'

A smile was wavering at the marshal's lips. He said, 'What a guy. He took them on right there at the airport?'

'Took 'em on, hell. Practically shot them out of the sky. Demolished the plane, killed eighteen, hurt a bunch more. The brothers came out with scratches. . . .'

'That's a bit much,' the marshal commented, his lips flattening against his teeth. 'The guy is going rocky, Hal.'

The group of lawmen were moving along the flight line to the transport section. Brognola heaved a deep sigh and said, 'I don't know. I've never known Bolan to be fast and loose with the civilians. He's usually pretty careful about that – always, in fact. It may be significant to note that there was absolutely no other traffic – not on the ground, not over the field, not even in the entire control zone.'

'It still sounds rocky. When he starts going after airplanes . . .'

'What's so damned sacred about an airplane?' the justice official snapped testily. 'A target is a target to the guy, so long as the civilians are clear and safely out of it.'

The marshal grinned and said, 'Hell, I didn't know you cared.'

'Well I do, and I guess it's no secret. I've tried everything to . . . but orders are orders – and believe me, I'll put a bullet in his head as fast as not. I just like to keep the perspectives in mind, that's all.'

'I like the guy myself, Hal. But that can't change anything.'

'Not a thing,' Brognola agreed.

'We'll gun the poor S.O.B. down just like we would any lunatic. Right?'

'Right,' Brognola calmly replied, refusing to be baited.

The party had reached the helicopter area. The marshal stepped back to allow the other man to board first. 'Even though we know he'll never return our fire,' he said quietly. 'Right?'

'You'd better hope not,' Brognola muttered. He climbed into the aircraft and turned back to add, 'I've seen the guy's work. He's a real classy sharpshooter, make no mistakes. And he goes for the head.'

'I won't make any mistakes,' the chief marshal replied. 'We have a few sharpshooters in our troop too, you know.'

Brognola sighed and dropped into a seat. 'That's the only damn reason you're here.'

Indeed. It was the 'only damn reason' Brognola himself was there. He'd been the guy's champion. Now, as the official closest to the problem, it was logical – if ironic as hell – that he be given the task of eliminating the problem.

As for Bolan shooting back . . . Brognola knew damn

well that he would not. A more distasteful chore had never arisen during a career often sadly lacking in taste. But . . . it was the way things were.

He had to get Bolan. He simply had to get him.

CHAPTER ELEVEN

THE WATCH

THE Vegas Strip has a 'grapevine' second to none in the world. Despite efforts by both police and underworld to quiet the fact of the Executioner's presence in town, the word spread among the regular residents with the vigor of an uncontrolled forest fire.

The incident at the airport, together with the executions on the Strip itself and the invasion of Gold Duster earlier that morning, became the chief topic of hushed conversation in the twenty-four hour city. These inevitably led to a rehashing of the Bolan legend, much of it inaccurate or exaggerated.

'The guy has a CIA license to kill.' This was the favourite story.

As close runner up, 'He's got a thousand faces, and nobody really knows what he looks like.'

'Just watch,' went another attention getter, 'when he's finished, the cops will step in and mop up his leavings.'

The consensus of opinion in the law-abiding community was heavily sympathetic to Bolan. All of the professionals in Vegas knew, of course, which were the mob joints and which were not – this also was a perennial favorite topic of conversation. Most of the 'straights' had adopted a live and let-live attitude toward the mob – this was the Vegas tradition. It was no secret, however, that the legitimate casino operators resented the unfair advantage which naturally fell to the kinky businessmen through their connections in high places and a virtually unlimited supply of financial support. So the straight people of Vegas were shedding no tears over the Bolan crusade, except for the fear that it might depress the tourist situation.

Just the same, there was a noticeable apprehension all along the Strip and in the city's Glitter Gulch – wherever games were played in that valley. Dealers flipped their cards with one eye on the table and the other on the door. Pit bosses nervously scrutinized unfamiliar faces and security personnel strolled about with hands resting on pistol butts.

The city's visitors, assiduously kept 'out of the know' by the regulars, remarked upon the number of police vehicles cruising the Strip and the hordes of foot patrolmen on Fremont Street, particularly in Glitter Glulch. If one were to look carefully he might note that some of these officers were from other areas adjacent to Las Vegas – such as North Las Vegas, East Vegas, Henderson, and even from Boulder City. A person with a practiced eye for concealed weapons could possibly discern the presence also of great numbers of alert guntoters in civilian clothing, although the observer would need a great instinct for separating the good guys from the bad.

And all about Las Vegas – the city of strangers – faces suddenly became highly important, almost an obsession, for those who lived and worked there. Police accosted everyone who seemed to stand out a little from the crowd; frequently they accosted one another. Hardfaced men in tailored silk suits and dark glasses stood in hotel lobbies and prowled the lounges and the casinos, also 'accosting' anyone who aroused their suspicious natures and here, also, the frequent mutual stare-downs and violent reactions between accoster and accosted would have been comical, if not so potentially tragic. A minor shoot-out did occur in a Fremont Street tavern between two men who were later identified as 'free-lancers', bounty hunters seeking the pot of gold in Bolan's head.

In this latter regard, special police details were stationed at the airport and in bus and train depots to turn back an expected invasion of gunmen, both free-lance and otherwise.

The 'Bolan Watch' was on, and if the atmosphere in the civilian community was tense, it was downright explosive in the police and underworld segments.

It was leaked in the press, for example, that a special federal 'strike force' was in town and that a highly placed official in the Justice Department was coordinating all police efforts in the matter. There were rumors of hard feelings among the local cops, and a wire-press reporter in Carson City, the state capital, charged that state and federal officials had clamped a 'news blackout' on the events at Las Vegas.

Rumors of a different nature began flowing from the Gold Duster when Vito Apostinni 'didn't show up for the noon count'. The story that swept along the Strip claimed that 'Heart o' Gold Vito got planted in Skeleton Flats', this latter a reference to the unofficial graveyard supposedly existing in the desert somewhere along Highway 91, far south of the city.

It was also being said that eastern bigshots had taken over the entire top floor of the Gold Duster Hotel and that the whole place had become an armed camp, with much coming and going on the part of the area's criminal element. Those 'in the know' whispered about an underworld purge in the western crime capital, and the stories became more persistent as the day wore on.

Bolan himself seemed unperturbed by the commotion. He had gone directly from the dawn strike at the airport to his modest tourist-home accommodations on the north side. After a leisurely meal in his room and a shower, he went to bed for a refreshing six-hour sleep.

At two o'clock he was on the move again, dressed casually in modish flair slacks, sport shirt, and bright blue blazer. He walked through Glitter Gulch, the gambling center of the downtown area, and fed slot machines at several of the joints. He kept his ears open and his nose clean, and after an hour of this 'scouting', he invaded the

Strip via taxicab and went directly to the hotel where he had met Tommy Anders and the Ranger Girls some hours earlier.

He scouted the parking lot, decided that the watch on his wheels had been lifted, reclaimed his Pontiac and set out on a tour of the neon jungle's high spots.

The Executioner had, many death-waits ago, learned to blend into a given environment and to become a part of the background of almost any situation.

A 'watch' could work in more directions than one.

The watchers themselves were being watched.

CHAPTER TWELVE

CRAP OUT

At nightfall, Bolan returned to his room and again changed clothes. He donned the black skinsuit and covered it with the dark silk tailormade threads favored by big time torpedoes, beneath the coat a pastel shirt with flaring collar and oversized tie and – the trusty Beretta in sideleather.

He fussed with his hair to achieve the just right look, then put a band-aid across the bridge of his nose and another just off the chin along the jawline. Purple tinted lenses in gold wire frames and a black rollbrim hat completed the job to his satisfaction.

Then he went directly to the Gold Duster.

A congregation of hoods and uniformed deputies stood outside, eyeing everyone who passed.

The smirking Bolan flipped them a bird as he swaggered through the cluster. One of the men behind him muttered, 'Wise ass.'

Bolan jerked around and quietly demanded, 'Who said that?'

None responded or even returned the hard stare. He sniggered and proceeded to the lobby.

'Boys' were all over the place, several of them almost identical in appearance to the new arrival. Band-aids sprouted freely, here and there a head-wrap, and a guy going into the lounge was showing a pronounced limp.

Bolan felt right at home.

He went straight to the desk, elbowed an elderly lady

out of the way, and commanded the immediate attention of a room clerk.

'Are they still upstairs?' he asked the guy.

The clerk nodded his head uncertainly and replied, 'Uh, yes sir, I think so.'

'Check!' Bolan demanded.

'Uh, come to think of it,' the clerk suddenly remembered, 'they are. We just sent up dinner.'

The guy started to turn away. Bolan leaned across the desk and grabbed his arm. 'Get Hard Mountain for me.'

'Sir?'

'I got a friend out there. Make the call, eh?'

The clerk nervously pulled loose from Bolan's grasp and said, 'Yes sir.' His eyes fled to a corner area of upholstered chairs and mahogany tables. 'You can take the call in the telephone lounge, sir. Just pick up the receiver, I'll have the switchboard put you through.'

Bolan growled, 'Thanks,' and threw the guy a fiver.

The light was on when he reached the house phone. He picked it up and said, 'Yeah, who's this?'

'I'm ringing, sir,' the operator reported.

'Oh yeah, okay. When they answer, honey, you get the hell off. This is private.'

'Certainly, sir,' the house operator assured him in an offended tone.

'Don't mention it,' he said.

A few seconds later she told him, 'Go ahead, sir. I'm *leaving*.'

He snickered into the transmitter and said, 'Who's this?'

A guarded male voice replied, 'This is Desert High Ranch. Who'd you want?'

Bolan chuckled and asked, 'Been laid lately?'

The guy chuckled back. 'At *this* goddam joint? Hey who's this?'

'This is Vinton.'

'Who?'

'You know. I came in this morning.' Bolan snickered. 'By the skin of my teeth, I mean.'

The guy laughed. 'I know what you mean. That bastard hit up here, too, last night.'

'Yeah I heard,' Bolan said chattily. 'We're at the Duster, you knew that.'

'Yeah. Uh, who'd you want?'

'Shit, he didn't say who I should call, he just said call.'

'Who said? Joe?'

'Yeh. I guess I oughta talk to the head cock-in-charge, eh?'

The guy laughed again and said, 'I guess you're talking to 'im. This's Red Evans.'

'That don't sound kosher to me,' Bolan said lightly.

'I guess it's about as kosher as Vinton, eh?' The guy was obviously enjoying the conversation. 'I could give you about a dozen different calling cards, if you wanted 'em all that bad.'

'Listen, I gotta come out there, I guess.'

'Yeah sure, you're welcome. Bring about a dozen broads too, huh?'

Bolan laughed and said, 'I'm looking at a six foot Swede right now. Legs about four feet long, squeeze you until you scream for mercy. I think I'll lay her 'fore I come out.'

'What's her name?'

'Shit, who cares?' Bolan snickered. 'All ass and tits. Dumbest looking broad I ever saw.'

'Stop it, you're talking to a fuckin' monk. I been up here six days straight. Supposed to get rotated back to town today, then this son of a bitch comes roaring into town. Why're you coming out?'

'That's what I called about. You're supposed to go down and find that shipment.'

'What?'

'That heist that wasn't a heist. It's still out there.'

'Bullshit,' the guy said calmly. 'I don't know what you're talking about.'

'I'm talking about the shipment this guy was supposed to've lifted. He didn't.'

'He didn't what?'

'He didn't get it.'

'Bullshit, who says so. Is Joe—'

'Sure, what the hell you think? We got a turkey that ain't shut up for an hour now.'

'No shit!'

'Yeah. The stuff's out there, somewhere, on the side of that hill.'

'No shit!'

'Yeh. Joe says to send those guys down lookin' for it.'

'You mean these . . .?'

'Yeh, the figure boys. They didn't up and leave, did they?'

'Course not. When Joe says stay, they stay. Well look. . . .'

'How many boys you got left out there, Red?'

'Well not many. I don't like softing the joint. I mean, if that guy comes back. . . .'

'Nah, he's holing up somewheres. Hell, we got this town so heavy a guy can't hardly breathe.' Bolan chuckled. 'Everything's stopped dead 'cept the roll of the dice and slap slap slap of the cardboards.'

'When that stops, I'm getting off,' the guy replied, laughing.

'Me too.'

'Well where are we supposed to look?'

'Straight down the hill from where the hit was. This guy says they just got tossed overboard, so look straight down the hill.'

'I guess that turkey's name ain't Bolan, huh?'

'I wish it was.'

'Me too,' the guy said glumly. 'Listen, there's only four of us. I mean, except for the button-down collars.'

'They don't count,' Bolan agreed.

'They sure don't.'

'They try to jump up each other's asses at the first snap of a trigger.'

The hardman laughed. 'That's right.'

'It won't hurt 'em to do a little midnight mountain climbing. Right?'

The suggestion broke the guy up. Some seconds later he gasped, 'I wish I could go out and watch 'em.'

'Don't,' Bolan cautioned. 'You stay in the joint.'

'Yeah I will, but I wish I could.'

'I wish I could bring you a couple dozen broads, Red. You sound like an okay guy.'

'Yeah, you too. Listen, when you coming out?'

'Soon as I can take care of a few things here first. You know. Listen, this is what Joe says, not me. Keep this quiet.'

'Oh sure.'

'As of this minute right now, you talk to nobody.'

'Oh sure, right.'

'You got my name? Vinton. Remember it. You talk to nobody else.'

'I got it, Vinton, yeah. Don't worry.'

The guy definitely was beginning to sound worried, though.

'Get that chopper warmed up,' Bolan commanded. 'And keep it ready. Things are getting hot down here. You-know-who just might need a quick way out.'

'Oh . . . you mean . . . a *couple* of you-know-whos.'

'That's it.'

'Oh yeah, say. Do you know them personal?'

'What the hell?'

'Oh sure, I'm sorry.'

'That's okay. You're okay, Red.'

'Thanks. I'm sorry if I sounded. . . .'

'Oh hell no, that's okay. Listen. Maybe I should. . . .'

'Huh? What was you gonna say?'

'You sound like an okay guy.'

'Oh, well thanks.'

'Listen.'

'Yeah?'

'Your boss is . . . well, how do I put this?'

The voice from Hard Mountain was becoming more troubled by the moment. 'You mean the carpet, yeah, we all been wondering about that.'

'Well, you-know-who didn't 'preciate that stuff down at McCarran this morning.'

'Oh God, I guess not. God that was terrible.'

'Listen. Just a word, eh? Cool it with Joe.'

'Oh God yeah, thanks Mr. Vinton.'

'Don't uh, don't say anymore to him than you have to. You know? Just yes and no and that's all. You know?'

'God yes, I know. Don't worry. I won't.'

'Okay. Talk to me, and that's all.'

'Pardon me, but Joe didn't tell you to call, did he.'

'You got me, Red. He didn't.'

'God, we were all wondering about that.'

'You'll be okay, Red, don't worry.'

'Hell I appreciate—'

'Don't mention it. Send those jerks down the hill. If they find the stuff, just cool it. Sit tight. I'll be along soon as I can.'

'Oh sure. Are you, uh, bringing a force out?'

'I'm thinking about it.' Bolan chuckled. 'Who'd you say is the head cock out there?'

'Hey, uh, if you mean what I think you mean. . . .'

'Yeah, you know what I mean,' Bolan assured him.

'Listen, don't you worry about a thing. I'm in charge of this joint until you say otherwise.'

'I'll see you, Red.'

'Sure thing, Mr. Vinton. Sure thing.'

Bolan hung up and lit a cigarette, blowing the smoke in a dense cloud toward the center of the lobby.

Nothing, he would have enjoyed telling Red-the-head-cock, is ever a sure thing. Nothing. But that was no reason to quit trying.

Bolan never quit trying.

He got up and went into the lounge and ran full-body into Toby Ranger and her Canuck side-kick, the body-lover.

'Pardon me, honey,' he apologized nastily. 'You should look out where I'm going.'

He went on to the bar without looking back.

He knew, though, that the two girls were still standing in the doorway, watching him.

He threw a five spot on the bar and loudly demanded service.

For double-dam sure, there was no such thing as a sure thing.

It looked as though his dice had come up aceydeucey. It was a crap-out.

CHAPTER THIRTEEN

NATURAL

BOLAN had not set the stage in Vegas. Others had. And the man from blood was a superb opportunist who would grab any handle, twist any combination, and push on any door which might tend to equalize the staggering odds in his game of war and survival.

The situation in Vegas at that moment was heavily weighted against mere survival for Bolan. Any suggestion that he could not only survive but also score some degree of victory seemed unthinkable. But he would snatch at those handles, massage the combinations, and lunge against those doors until something worked . . . or until he suddenly dropped dead.

His greatest hope lay in the stage set for him by the forces intent on destroying him. The confusion and tension in the town was monumental, and he meant to play that angle for all it was worth.

But now here was Toby Ranger approaching him, in the enemy's heartland. One wrong word, a single suspicious gesture, anything at all which could seem out of place could mean his unmasking . . . and his total undoing.

She sidled up beside him at the bar and said, 'Buy a girl a drink, honey?'

Without turning his head, Bolan loudly replied, 'I already been laid twice today. Beat it!'

He felt her stiffen. The other girl moved in on his other side and placed everything she had against him.

He said, 'Whatsa matter? Business all that bad?'

The Canadian laughed softly and said, 'You're a riot, did anybody ever tell you that?'

No one seemed to be giving any attention to the little comedy at the bar, but Bolan figured that couldn't last forever. He tasted his drink, set it down, and hissed, 'Thanks, kids. You're all I needed.'

'Just keep it up, you're doing fine,' the blonde told him. 'We may even take you into our act.'

He growled, 'Yeah, Little Leddo, the lead-stuffed dummy. Bug off, eh?'

'We're looking for Tommy,' the body-bumper told him.

'I don't have him,' Bolan assured her.

'Somebody has,' the blonde said.

Bolan picked up his drink and yelled, '*A hundred bucks? What is it, gold-plated or something?*'

Toby's face turned fiery red.

Bolan laughed loudly and said, 'Awright, let's talk it over.'

He took the blonde's elbow and steered her away from the crowd at the bar and to a booth at the rear. The other girl followed close behind. Bolan slid into the booth and left the girls standing there. 'Siddown, siddown,' he said grandly.

Toby flounced in and angrily whispered, 'I should blow the whistle on you, you smart—'

'Shut up!' Bolan snapped. He told the Canadian, 'Siddown!'

She did.

He told them, 'This is no show biz stand, kids. When this curtain falls, it's a shroud. Now what's this about Anders?'

The Canuck was rubbing his arm. Toby Ranger's face was still set into angry lines. She said, 'He's been missing since five o'clock. We tracked him here. And suddenly the trail ends.'

'Did he come alone?' Bolan wanted to know.

'No. Two other men were with him.'

Bolan said, 'Okay, I'll find him.'
'Gee thanks.'
'Isn't that what you want me to do?'
'Well, sure,' the Canadian put in.
Bolan was staring at the blonde. Her eyes fell. 'I'm sorry,' she said. 'I guess it is a pretty dry stand, isn't it.'
He said, 'You know it.'
'Well, you look great,' she assured him.
'Didn't fool you,' he said.
'I'm special,' she replied, smiling.
'Yeah, you are at that,' he told her.
She colored again and glanced at the darkhaired girl. 'We'd better leave him alone, I guess.'
The Canuck said, 'You swim divinely.'
He told her, 'I bleed the same way. Where are the other girls?'
The blonde replied. 'We're supposed to go on in an hour. They're getting the costumes ready.'
Bolan said, 'Well, I'll nose around and find our man. But you girls beat it out of this joint. It's full of poison.'
'Okay,' the blonde replied meekly.
Bolan left them there and went into the casino. The action there was light and listless. The help seemed up-tight and jittery. Less than a hundred people were at the tables. Another twenty or so were feeding slots at the back wall.
Bolans' quick visual sweep disclosed maybe a dozen hoods, all locals if his instincts were still operative. He wondered about that and decided that the casino had been placed off-limits to the visiting torpedoes.
Somewhere in that crowd, also – Bolan was sure – would be a goodly representation from various police branches.
Across the partition, in the dining room, a show was getting underway with a fanfare from the band – muffled, in the casino, so as not to distract the more important business at the tables.

Bolan stopped at a craps table which was enjoying a small flurry of action. He threw a twenty at the croupier. The guy pushed him a stack of chips and announced, 'The cubes are hot.'

'I'll bet,' Bolan growled.

He watched the up-man bounce the dice across the table for a pair of threes.

The point is six,' the house man announced.

Bolan pushed his stack of chips into play and proclaimed, 'He makes it.'

'House covers.'

The guy rolled a seven and cried, 'Aw shit!'

'Craps,' announced the croupier.

'It figures,' Bolan sneered, and walked away.

The stairway to Vito's joint was blocked by a couple of hardmen. Bolan went straight to them and said, 'Is he there?'

The gunners looked him over and one of them replied, 'Yeh, he's there.'

'Run up and tell 'im I wanta see 'im.'

A muscle popped in the guy's jaw. He said, 'Fuck you, and run up yourself.'

Bolan sniggered. 'You boys out here don't take no shit, do you?' he commented.

'Not usually,' the guy said.

Bolan grinned and went on up the stairs.

A little guy in shirtsleeves occupied a chair at the landing. He looked at the visitor and asked, 'Where ya going, stud?'

'Run in there and tell the man I want 'im,' Bolan demanded, recognizing Max Keno.

'*Who* wants him?'

'Vinton.'

'I don't know ya, Vinton.'

'You will, Max. You will.'

'Oh, well . . . you wanta see him?'

'I didn't walk all the way up here to see *you*, dumdum.'

The little guy smiled and said, 'Ain't it a hell of a day? You hurt much?'

Bolan rubbed his jaw and said, 'Nah, I still got my swinger, I guess that's all that counts.'

Keno laughed and told Bolan, 'Just push the button on the door there. They'll let you in.'

'Who's in there besides him?'

'Aw, that wop, the comic. They're still sweating him.'

'That's really why I came,' Bolan confided. 'They think he should've broken down long ago.'

'Well, Joe figures it's better to last it longer and get it better, he ain't getting too rough. Vito got carried away yesterday on the other guy.'

'And now Vito gets carried away,' Bolan said, his voice dropping low.

'Yeh, I hate that. I was with Vito three years. He was okay to me. I hated that.'

Bolan sighed. 'Don't worry, we all did, even you-know-who. Well. . . .' He shrugged and smiled philosophically. 'That's the way it goes sometimes. We never know, do we, Max? I just push the button, eh?'

'Yeh. Just a minute, I'll . . .' The little tagman heaved out of the chair and went over to work the local lockworks for the out-of-towner.

What the hell. The guy could turn out to be his next boss, who could know?

He pressed the intercom signal and said, 'It's Vinton. He wants in.'

'Who?' came the reply.

'You know. Vinton. He's with . . . you know.'

The buzzer sounded and the door popped open. Bolan strolled in, noting that Vito's elaborate security jazz had been abandoned. The tower was not manned, there were no spotlights.

Joe Stanno was stretched out on a couch, asleep.

Tommy Anders occupied a swivel chair in the center of the room. Two guys sat facing him, another was perched atop the desk, just behind the comic. It was this one who challenged Bolan.

'Whattaya want in here?' he growled.

Bolan ignored him.

Anders looked like hell. His hair was in his face and his head was lying back on his shoulders as though his neck couldn't hold it up any longer. He was tied to the chair. There was no visible evidence of acts of violence suffered, but Bolan knew.

He went over to stand beside the couch and glare down at Stanno. 'What the hell is he doin' sleeping?' he snarled.

'Oh, did he forget to get a chit?' the guy at the desk said, with a voice heavy with sarcasm.

There were bad feelings here, very bad feelings, between the locals and the nationals.

Bolan caressed the band-aid at his nose and rubbed a bit of salt. 'Did he have a chat at the airport this morning?'

The guy lunged forward and slapped the back of Anders' head, taking it out on him.

The comic's head snapped to the other side and he quickly picked it up. He stared dully at Bolan and said, very distinctly, 'Fuck you.'

Bolan snickered and said, 'Shit, I didn't pop you, guy.'

'It still goes,' Anders muttered.

'He don't like anybody,' Bolan said, grinning.

'He's a smart ass!' the guy at the desk growled, and slapped the helpless man again. 'Plays cute games with cops and a certain bastard.'

Bolan again looked toward Stanno. 'That guy will sleep through anything,' he said. 'Wake 'im up.'

'You don't wake 'im up!' the headslapper growled. 'He was up all night and all day. Now leave 'im alone.'

'Sure, I'll leave 'im alone,' Bolan said quietly.

'So whattaya want in here?'

'They sent me.' He went over and rubbed Anders' scalp

with his knuckles. 'They say you've had the guy long enough. They wanta talk to 'im awhile. This guy is our only handle.'

'We ain't sure about that!'

'Well when do you figure on getting sure? He was right there when two of your own boys got it, wasn't he!'

'We're working 'im the right way,' the guy stubbornly maintained.

'You *was*,' Bolan corrected him in a soft voice.

The two guys in the chairs stood up abruptly. The one at the desk slid off and walked around the chair to show Bolan a fierce scowl. 'I've seen you somewheres, Vinton,' he declared.

'You're going to be seeing me a lot,' Bolan promised, scowling back.

'Yeah?'

'On second thought, maybe not. You're so cozy with sleeping beauty there, maybe I'll just let you *stay* with 'im.'

The guy sent a suddenly worried glance to his two companions. He said, 'Well now wait. Just what the hell . . .?' His gaze slid to Stanno and back to Bolan. His face tightened and he said, 'Yeah?'

Quietly, Bolan said, 'That's the way it goes.'

The two other inquisitors were shuffling their feet about and giving each other significant looks. The spokesman for the trio dropped his voice to a quiet murmur and said, 'Well, that's a hell of a note.'

In the language of the mob, Joe Stanno's death had just been announced as imminent.

'That's the way it goes,' Bolan said again. 'You can't do nothing for a leper, you know that, so don't go getting all busted up. Go on downstairs and find something to do. Better than that, get lost for a couple of hours.'

'Oh Christ no,' the guy groaned, the message just now fully reaching home. 'Has it actually got to that?'

'You in love with the guy or something?'

'Well no . . . but . . . we been together a long time.'

'So you won't want to be around for the next couple of hours,' Bolan suggested.

'How the hell can they just decide something like that with the snap of a finger?' the loyal crewchief whispered loudly.

'You wanta go up there and ask them?' Bolan said, the voice now hard and cold.

The guy backed off. His face moved into composed lines and he said, 'Forget I said that, huh?'

Bolan shrugged and replied, 'I didn't even hear it. Go on, cut out. I'll take care of your peon here, too.'

The guy squared his shoulders, took a long look at the sleeping man on the couch, then marched quickly from the room. The other two followed close behind. The door closed and Bolan went to work at the sashcord on Anders' wrist.

The comic said, 'I'm not no ethnician, but you Wops live lousy lives.'

'I'm a Polack,' Bolan said, using his own voice.

'I don't care if you're a . . .' The little man's eyes were opening wider and he was taking his first good look.

Bolan grinned and told him, 'Come on, you're going to be late for your first show.'

'Hell God, it's you!' the comic whispered.

'I thought the other guy knew it too, for a minute there,' Bolan confided. He jerked the ropes away and pulled Anders to his feet. 'Can you walk okay?' he asked him.

'Can a jackrabbit jump?' Anders smoothed his hair and straightened his clothing. 'I could walk out of *this* place with two broken legs and a splinted dick.'

Bolan chuckled and pushed the comic ahead of him to the door. 'Keep it straight until we're clear and running,' he cautioned.

'What about Stanno?'

'Let Stanno worry about himself,' Bolan said.

They went out and Bolan carefully closed the door.

Max Keno was sitting sideways in his chair. He gave

Bolan a scared look and said, 'What the hell is going on?'

'Nothing you have to worry about,' Bolan told him. 'Just don't go opening no doors until I give the word. Not for nobody.'

'Hell no, I won't, the little tagman assured him.

'For *no*body.'

'Right, that's right, boss.'

Bolan grinned and touched Keno's chin with his knuckles, then he interlocked arms with Anders and led him down the stairs.

'I've had enough,' the comic told him in low voice. 'If you can't keep the ants out of the picnic basket, then you might as well give up the picnic.'

'You're throwing in the towel?' Bolan asked, scowling out upon the casino floor.

'I'm getting out. Time to retire, I guess.'

'A priest can't retire, Anders.'

'What priest? Who said anything—'

'If the mob is the invisible second government in this country, then your business is the invisible second church.'

They reached the bottom of the stairs, now unblocked and no sign of the two who'd been there earlier.

Anders was saying, 'You wouldn't say that if you'd played the dumps I have.'

'It'd be a damn gray world if everybody in your business closed up shop.'

They were moving across the casino floor, Bolan looking neither left nor right.

'I guess that's right,' the comic said.

'It's true and you know it. That's why the biz captures anybody who brushes it. It's where the soul is, and you know it. It's where *your* soul is, Anders, and that's why you're straining so hard to keep the ratpacks out.'

'Maybe you're right. I never thought of myself as a priest, though. How'd you find me?'

Bolan fiercely stared down a pair of gunners who momentarily blocked his path. The guys gave way and Bolan pushed his man on through.

'How'd you find me?' Anders asked again.

Bolan kept his scowl intact and said, 'A couple of unholy sisters showed me the way. I believe they would've gone after you themselves if they'd known exactly where to go.'

'What're you talking about?'

But Bolan did not have to answer the question.

The two girls were waiting in the lobby and trying to ignore the ogling attention of the guys in the silk suits.

Bolan gave Anders a hard shove and propelled him into the girls. 'Get outta here!' he yelled. 'And take your gold-plated sluts with you! I catch you peddling flesh in here again and I'll run you clear outta town!'

The twenty odd people milling around in there froze and interestedly watched the disturbance as the big 'torpedo' advanced menacingly on the trio. 'I said *get out*!' he yelled, the voice hard and threatening.

They got out, and the cluster of men near the doorway hastily parted ranks to let them through.

'That's how it's going to be around here from now on!' Bolan proclaimed to everybody within hailing distance, then he turned around and stalked back into the casino.

That took care of Anders and the girls.

Now all he had to do was complete this mission and get himself out.

For the moment, at least, he was rolling nothing but naturals.

CHAPTER FOURTEEN

NEW BLOOD

TIME was of the essence now, and Bolan swept through the casino, loudly collaring the pit bosses and dragging them along with him. He was 'high-rolling' with everything of value to his life, plus his life itself, in the stakes on destiny's crap table.

The guys were murmuring among themselves as they tagged along, and snatches of the comments were reaching Bolan's alert ears.

'I dunno, he just said . . .'

'. . . for the new owners I guess . . .'

'Hell who knows what to expect next around this . . .?'

'. . . name's Vinton, I think. I don't . . .'

'Vinton' halted the procession at the foot of the stairway to Vito's ex-joint and yelled up to the tagman.

'Max!'

'Yes, boss?'

'Round up some boys and show everybody the door. We're closing at the eight count.'

A pit boss in the Bolan entourage groaned, 'Whaaat?'

Keno was scampering down the stairway and fighting his way into his coat. Bolan told him, 'Pass the word they can come back at midnight. Meanwhile everything in the lounge and dining-room is on the house. And I want a continuous floor show! Nothin' stops but the action in the pits!'

Keno chirped, 'Yes *sir*!' and hurried off on his mission.

A pit boss standing at Bolan's elbow reminded him, 'We're just going into a shift-change, Mr. uh . . .'

Bolan snapped, 'Mr. *Vinton* and you better remember it. Listen, you run back and tell the new shift what I just said. It's on the house for them too. They go to work at midnight.'

The guy grinned and said, 'Sure, Mr. Vinton,' and took off.

The procession moved on to the counting rooms and offices at the rear of the building, Bolan bulldozing his way through the most elaborate security network on the Strip.

The people in the rear had been making preparations for the eight o'clock count, due very shortly. Bolan invited them all to sit down, and he shoved the pit bosses into a line against the wall and began his speech.

'I guess you all know by this time what's going on,' he said, positive that they did not. 'You all heard that Mr. Apostinni cashed out and moved on, but it ain't going to be legal until midnight. We gotta close this joint out, and I mean tidy. You get me? *Tidy*!

'So we're knocking off all the action, starting right now. I want all the table stakes brung in and counted, all of it, everything. No goddam balance sheets, understand? Counted! You got four hours, you hear me? – four fucking hours, pardon me ladies, to tidy this place up for the new management. I don't want a nickel left out. Who the hell is the boss in charge of the count?'

A nervous man in goldrimmed spectacles stepped forward and identified himself as 'the controller'.

'Awright, you control it then,' Bolan growled. 'We clear it out and then start over clean at midnight with a whole new deal. You got that?'

The controller assured the 'new boss' that he had that.

Bolan swung a fierce gaze to the pit bosses. 'Are you guys coming on or going off?' he asked.

'Going off,' one of them replied.

'Wrong,' Bolan said. 'You're staying to help out. Don't worry, you're getting paid. Grab the other guys when they come in and break the work. When you get everything cleared out and turned over to these ladies back here, go enjoy yourself on the house.'

The controller then hesitantly ventured to observe that it was customary and perfectly acceptable to open new books on the records obtained from the routine counts.

The 'new boss' informed the controller, in no uncertain terms, that he did not give a good shit what was customary and that everyone would be wise to do precisely as they were told.

There were no more objections, and no questions. Bolan herded the pit bosses back to the casino floor and turned them loose. Their attitudes were now entirely jovial. It was all smiles and smirks, and Bolan's parting shot to them was, 'It's gonna be a lot better around here from now on!'

Not a man present doubted the truth of that.

Vito had been a hard taskmaster.

Mr. Vinton was tough, sure, but an okay guy. Not once in sixteen years had anything, either crumb or sip, been served up 'on the house' at the Duster.

The place was emptying, over the loud objections of several 'hot' patrons.

Bolan climbed half of the stairs and yelled, 'If they don't wanta leave, *throw* 'em out!'

He caught Max Keno's eye, down on the floor, and motioned him to front and center.

'You're on me now, Max,' he told the tagman.

'You bet I am, boss,' the little guy told him with a smile.

Instant loyalty. It was the name of the Mafia game. Off with the old and in with the new.

Max dropped into his chair and 'Mr. Vinton' went into his new joint – which, briefly, he would be sharing with a certain sleeping beauty.

The time was 8.20 and Joe Stanno was still asleep. Bolan had been quietly going through the desk and pocketing various useful items of intelligence.

He selected an entry from a list of telephone numbers, leaned against the front of the desk to keep an eye on his unconscious companion, and made a call.

'Hello, this is Vinton, who's this?' he announced as soon as the receiver was lifted on the other end.

The quietly jubilant tones of Red Evans crowded the line. 'We found it, Mr. Vinton, we got the stuff.'

'That's great,' Bolan said, his manner entirely business-like now. 'Is it all there?'

'Yessir we think so. Two cases, we found both of 'em. The button-collars are counting it right now. But it looks all there.'

'Here's what you do. Red. You get the stuff counted, and you get two witnesses to the tally. I mean, other than the jerks. Two of your own boys, right?'

'Right, I gotcha.'

'Then you tell me the – who's the head jerk?'

'Oh that's Lemke, L-E-M-K-E, Lemke.'

'*That* guy. Okay, here's what I want Lemke to do. He sets up a whole new route, I mean everything right down to the final stop. He tells nobody, but *no*body, what that route is, not even the pilot. Then he puts that stuff in the chopper, and just hisself and the pilot. You got all that?'

'I got it, Mr. Vinton.'

'He leaves the other jerks right there, 'cause we're going to need that room in the chopper.'

'Oh yeah, I gotcha.'

'He keeps that route a national secret, now. Our you-know-who's will drop out whenever they feel like it. But he keeps it quiet, you hear?'

'Oh sure, I understand that.'

'What time you got now, Red?'

'I got, let's see, it's eight-twenty-one.'

'Okay. You get Lemke's clock to ticking right with

yours, and you shove that chopper off out there in exactly twenty minutes. That would make that eight-forty-one. Right?'

'Uh, right Mr. Vinton.'

'You tell that jerk – who's that pilot?'

'That's Jack Grimaldi, Mr. Vinton. He's an okay guy.'

'Okay, you tell Jack I want that chopper settlin' down on this roof here at exactly nine o'clock. I don't mean a minute before or a minute after, I mean exactly nine o'clock. You got that?'

'On the top of the hotel boss?'

'No hell no, not the hotel, the casino.'

'Oh yeah, I gotcha.'

'He comes down on top of the joint.'

'Yessir, I got that.'

'That don't give you much time, so you better get busy.'

'Oh yeah, sure. Uh, you coming out tonight?'

'I might. I might not. Depends how things go. I guess it's in good hands out there, eh Red?'

'Oh, yes sir, you can count on that.'

'Right. Now you get busy.'

Bolan hung up and massaged his fist against his neck and stared glumly at his sleeping beauty.

Damn! The numbers were getting brutal!

The brothers had finished a six-course repast elegantly prepared by the self-proclaimed best chef on the Strip. It was their first meal of long and hard day, and now they were relaxing and unwinding taut nerves on the penthouse terrace with brandy and handrolled cigars.

'How long can this go on?' Pat wondered aloud.

'It'll break. Any minute it will break.' Mike assured his brother.

'I wish I could be that sure. I keep wondering if he's half-way to the border by now.'

'No, the guy's an ego-freak. He knows we're in town.

He knows he missed us at the airport. He'll be showing.'

'I wish Joe could get something out of the funny man.'

'I don't believe the funny man knows anything,' Mike said. 'If I did, I'd be talking to him myself – or I'd have him torn in half by now and gagging on his own cock.'

The other brother made a face and said, 'Not on a full stomach, my brother.'

A bodyguard on the roof railing chuckled and commented, 'Not on *any* stomach. Yuck.'

The brothers laughed and sipped their brandies.

Presently, Pat observed, 'Bolan doesn't leave many tracks.'

'Just all over our backs,' the other said, smiling.

'It's a hell of a way to fight a war. You wait until the guy rears up and pops at you. Then you try to pop him back before he disappears again.'

'Go tell it in Vietnam.'

They laughed again. 'You want to call it off?' Mike asked.

Pat Talifero snorted and got to his feet. 'Not until I take a bath in his blood,' he said.

They laughed again.

Pat went to the railing and stood beside the bodyguard to gaze down upon the neon jungle spreading in both directions away from their position. 'That's some battlefield,' he said. 'You know something? I hate this goddamned town. Always have. Don't they have an atom bomb testing place somewhere around here?'

The bodyguard said, 'Yessir.'

'They oughta have a mis-fire.'

Mike Talifero laughed 'What you need is a fresh lay. There's lots of talent around.'

'As long as that guy is alive,' Pat replied, 'it would be like playing with myself.'

'You swearing off for the duration?'

'Not hardly.'

Mike laughed some more, then told his brother, 'Well, tonight will be the night.'

'I wish I could be that sure,' the other said glumly. 'I just can't see the guy hanging around after what he did to us this morning.'

'Look, he'll hit again, I know he will. So stop beefing.'

'I hope it's soon. I want to get out of here.'

'It's the wrong foot we arrived on. I'd like to take that fuckin' Stanno and shove something up his ass. And I might. If the guy wasn't so damned *effective* . . .'

'*Most* of the time, you mean,' Pat said.

'Yeah, that's what I meant. Joe's okay, I guess.'

'Yeah, but one more fuck-up like this morning, and . . .'

'Right,' Mike agreed. 'The next is the last.'

Bodyguards were supposed to develop hearing problems during such candid moments. This one was gazing at the stars and totally out of the conversation.

'Remember Stiffy Peters?' Pat asked.

'They sometimes called him Shaker Sam,' Mike recalled.

'Right. He tried to pull that amnesia gag on old man Marinello.'

'That was that Bronx rumble,' Mike said.

They were laughing it up.

The bodyguard continued to stargaze, but put in with, 'I never did hear what became of Siffy.'

Still laughing, Mike told him, 'You never will, either. Not unless you can operate a jackhammer at the bottom of the Hudson.'

Pat sniggered and added, 'And you'd have to chip away two feet of concrete bathing suit.'

'Siffy Peters was a better hit man than Joe Stanno,' the bodyguard said. 'That is, until he got all conked up with the siff.'

'You think so?' Mike asked.

'That's what I think,' the guy replied.

A lieutenant stepped on to the terrace and stood quietly by the doorway, awaiting recognition of his presence.

Pat Talifero was leaning against the railing, staring straight at the new arrival. Presently he asked, 'What is it now?'

'Guy here to see you, boss. Guy runs the hotel.'

'What the hell does *he* want?'

'He says, just droppin in.'

'Tell him to just drop out. We got no time for – what's new from the street?'

'Glitter Gulch checked in, 'bout five minutes ago. Another zero.'

'Tell them to tighten up that damn sieve!'

'It's getting tougher all the time, boss. Cops are thick as flies out there.'

'I don't give a shit about the cops!' Pat Talifero yelled. 'How many places can a guy hide in this creep town? You tell those boys to – okay, send the jerk in.'

'Sir?'

'The hotel jerk, let's observe the formalities, I guess.'

'Yessir.'

The guy faded out.

'Those guys aren't trying hard enough!' Pat fumed. 'I believe they're all scared they *will* stumble on the guy!'

Mike shrugged and threw his cigar away. 'He'll stumble over us.'

'You keep saying that!'

'He will.'

A suave man of about forty appeared through the doorway. 'They told me I'd find you out here,' he said jovially.

Pat disliked the man instantly. He despised that soft pink pampered look some of these guys had. 'You found us,' he said. 'What do you want?'

'Just, uh, wanted to make sure you're comfortable and all.'

'And all what?'

The guy's face fell. He said, 'It's part of the VIP package, Mr. Talifero. I always look in on honored guests.'

'All right, you looked. Thanks. Goodbye.'

'I, uh . . .' The man took a step towards the doorway, then turned back and blurted, 'Do you know the new casino boss?'

'*What* new casino boss?'

'Well . . . I was wondering . . . he's setting up the house.'

'He *who*?'

'I believe the name is Vinton, a Mr. Vinton. It's the talk of the Strip, I wondered if you'd heard. He actually closed the casino.'

'*Closed* it?'

'Yes, until midnight. They're starting the new books at midnight. Until then, the drinks are on the house. And continuous entertainment. I just wondered if you knew.'

'Stop wondering, Mr. Crosser,' Mike said. 'Goodnight, Mr. Crosser.'

The guy murmured, 'Goodnight,' and took his leave.

The brothers stared at each other for a moment, then Mike said, 'Well, that was pretty quick. I passed the word east just a few hours ago.'

'They can move fast when they want to,' Pat replied, shrugging. 'You remember when Bugsy got his.'

'Sure, but that was set up,' Mike said. 'They had time to run someone in beforehand. But this time . . .'

'Maybe we should go talk to this new blood,' Pat said. 'He should check with us before he goes boarding up the place.'

'Why? That's not our action.'

'At a time like this, everything is our action.'

'May as well get a free drink anyway, eh?' the bodyguard said.

Mike frowned at that and declared, 'Hell, I don't want our boys sopping that stuff up.' He stood up, stretched, and rubbed his belly. 'I never heard of this Vinton. Did you?'

'Not by that name, no. Let's go talk to him.'

'Okay. But you'll find he's just another green felt jerk.'

'Maybe. Maybe not,' Pat said. He flipped his cigar over the railing, showed his brother a smile, and said, 'Let's go see.'

CHAPTER FIFTEEN

ALL BETS IN

BOLAN told the controller, 'Don't give me that noise! You pull it outta the goddam vault and you *count* it!'

'Mr. Vinton,' the flustered man protested, 'we have certified—'

'You shove your certifieds up your own ass, not mine!' Bolan roared. 'A new deal gets a new deck, don't it?'

'The house stakes, sir, are—'

Bolan grabbed the guy by the throat and shook him until his eyes were rolling. Then he threw him back against the wall. 'You're making me wonder, controller,' he said, in a voice quivering with pretended rage. 'Just what th' hell're you trying to cover up?'

'We'll count it, sir,' the terrified man agreed.

'I wanta see it with my own eyes, all 375-thou' of it. I wanta see it sitting there on the counting tables, and it better be there in ten minutes when I get down there! You hear me?'

The guy heard him.

Bolan growled, 'Now get outta here!'

The mob controller threw a last desperate look at the sleeping figure of Joe Stanno and hurried out, Bolan followed him to the door and called. 'Max!'

The tagman jerked around with a grin. 'Yes boss?'

'What time you got?'

'Uh . . . eight thirty, boss.'

'Right. At eight forty you remind me what time it is.'

'Sure boss.'

'I'm waking the sleeping beauty up now. You see he gets down the stairs okay.'

The smile broadened. 'Sure boss.'

Bolan closed the door, went over to the mirror and checked his appearance, put the hat on and rolled the brim down – then he went to the couch, grabbed one of Joe Stanno's big feet and he dragged the monster man onto the floor.

The FBI district chief leaned into the car and told Brognola, 'I've been looking all over for you. Where've been?'

'Prospecting,' the Justice official replied tiredly. 'Get in, Bill.'

'No, I'm taking a force to the Gold Duster. Something funny is going on down there.'

'All over this town,' Brognola said, sighing, 'something funny is going on.'

'Check up,' Miller said, grinning. 'The night is young. I thought you might want to check out the Duster with us.'

'What is it?'

'Well, you've heard the talk. it's all over the Strip.'

'Apostinni? Sure, I've heard. So what's new in funny-land?'

'One of my insiders at the Duster reports that the new boss has hit the scene. He's closed the casino until mid-night and he's setting up drinks all around.'

'That *is* funny,' Brognola commented.

'The funniest part is yet to be told. The guy's name is supposed to be Vinton. None of the mob watchers in these parts ever heard of the guy. My man says he looks more like an eastern torpedo than a syndicate jerk – you know, the silk suit cadre.'

Brognola nodded. 'The town's full of them.'

'Well . . .'

'It fits,' Brognola said, sighing. 'The hit on Vito was obviously a thing of the moment. So the brothers have obligingly put in a substitute until the next jerk shows up.'

'Well, there's one more thing,' Miller said. 'I know it sounds pretty far out but . . . well, my man says . . .'

'Yeah?'

'Hal, you're the Bolan expert. Would the guy try a stunt like *that*?'

'Like *what*?'

'Like masquerading as a guy called Vinton.'

Brognola stared silently at the other man for a long moment, then he replied, 'He sure would.'

'To what possible damned end?'

Brognola shrugged. 'Let's go ask him.'

'I mean, closing the joint and setting up drinks half the night . . . that sounds pretty flamboyant, even for Bolan.'

'He's a shrewd warrior,' Brognola said. 'Everything he does is to the numbers. How much of a force are you taking?'

'I've gathered up ten men.'

'You'd better gather up a lot more. What were you going to tell me? Something about your man at the Duster.'

'He says it's hard to get a good look at the guy. Vinton. He keeps moving, waves his arms around a lot, always seems to find a shadow for his face. Wearing lenses and bandages also. But he's the right size, the right build, and roughly the right age.'

'Uh, I'll get right down there,' Brognola said. 'You find my sidekick and tell him to get those marshals down there, *all* of them, and tell them to warm up their sharpshooter fingers. Get the locals to put a cordon around the place, very quietly, I mean like two men per square foot. Set up roadblocks. Send those horseback volunteers down there, too, semi-circle them on the desert side.'

'It's going to make us look awful damn silly if—'

'Don't worry about that, we'd look even sillier with

Bolan treating the town right beneath our noses. Anyway, my hackles are rising and I believe they're getting the Bolan scent.'

'The guy has pulled these wild stunts before, hasn't he?'

'You bet your badge he has. Remind me to tell you about Palm Springs some day.'

'Be careful, Hal.'

'Yeah.' Brognola threw the car into gear and screeched out of the parking lot with rubber burning.

Yeah. What a pity. What a hell of a rotten waste of a truly superior human being. Be careful. Those were not the right words, were they. Hell no. Be hard. Be hard, Hal, do your duty, and go gun down a very superior human being.

He would, of course. Because he had to. He and Bolan were two of a kind.

They simply did what they had to do.

Joseph Earl Stanno had not fallen off a bed since he was six years old. Of course it had been a hell of a bad day all the way around. One thing after another – the hit on the hill, the heist, eating shit from the Taliferis' plates, trying to run bastard Bolan to ground, the embarrassment at the Duster when the bastard rousted Vito – right under Joe's nose, then that Godawful hit at McCarran, the ordeal with Vito screaming and pleading for his life all during that long, hot desert ride . . . yeah, and it had been a rotten day all the way along, and without any sleep even. For thirty-six hours no damn sleep. No wonder he fell off the damn bed, he was probably having nightmares in his sleep as bad as they had been all day with his eyes wide open.

All this passed through his mind as he was struggling to get his swollen eyes opened, and he was thinking that, hell, he might never see again. Then he saw the pair of legs walking away from him, and he remembered where he was, and something swam up from his subconscious to make him realize that he hadn't fallen off – some bastard had *drug* him off.

Stanno rolled to his side and explored his face with probing fingers. The nose burned and it was throbbing some. He pulled his fingers away wet and warm and he knew that he was bleeding a little from his nose. What bastard had drug him off onto his nose?

He groaned and sat up, swaying drunkenly and wondering if he really was awake, after all. The guy perched there on the edge of the desk didn't look like anybody he knew personal, except for the expensive silk threads that a hundred guys he knew wore all the time.

Instinctively Joe's hand moved beneath his coat and came out empty. What bastard had relieved him of his hardware?

The guy at the desk was looking away from him, toward the wall, just sitting there and swinging his foot and staring off no where.

'Who the hell're you?' Stanno said in a raspy voice. 'What the hell is coming off?'

'I'm sorry, Mr. Stanno, I shouldn't be talking to you,' the guy said.

What the hell did he mean by that, why couldn't he talk to him? Shit, it was too hard to think about. His goddamn head was throbbing and he had that sick feeling in his gut, that hungry grabby feeling of not eating anything all night and all day.

Stanno struggled back to the couch. He pulled himself up and sat on the edge with his head in his hands.

The guy wasn't saying nothing.

Stanno looked up and asked him, 'Where's that guy?'

He just swung his foot and didn't say nothing.

'Didn't you hear me, you creep?' Joe the Monster yelled. 'Where's that guy, that smart-ass? Did he turkey out?'

Very quietly, the guy told him, 'That's old history, Mr.

Stanno. Look, you understand – nothing personal, I mean – but I can't afford to get heard talking to you.'

'What the hell d'you mean? *What* not talk to me? What old history?' The bewildered man lurched to his feet. 'Where's my rod?' he growled.

'Pardon me, but do you always wake up this hard?' the guy asked him. He slid off the desk and walked past, then returned and said, 'You look like hell, Mr. Stanno.'

And then the bastard threw a glass of cold water in Joe Stanno's face. It jerked him upright, though, and the red film in front of his eyes started going away, and his mind slipped into focus. And he knew with a terrible swiftness what the guy had been talking about.

'You don't wanta talk to me?' he asked, unable to accept the finality of *that* message.

'No sir, I'm sorry.'

'What the hell is going on?'

'You know, Mr. Stanno,' the guy told him.

Yeah, Stanno knew, how well he knew. How many times had he gone through this very same routine? How many times, and never ever believing that it would some day be coming back at him.

But . . . why? For God's sake, why? Shut up, Stanno, for God's bleating sake, shut up. You don't go out begging and screaming like Vito, *hell no.*

'They want to see you, Mr. Stanno,' the silksuit said.

'Oh is that right? And where are they?'

'Well you should know.'

'Don't get assy with *me*, boy.'

'No sir, I wouldn't.'

The kid was real polite. At least it was going to be dignified.

'I, uh, Christ I don't remember what's been going on, I guess, I mean I'm not woke up good yet. I was up thirty-six hours.'

'Yes sir.'

The guy came over and opened Joe's coat and dropped a rod into the leather. Quietly, amost sorrowfully, he said,

'I wouldn't send nobody out there naked, Mr. Stanno. Not my worst enemy.'

'Is that fuckin' thing loaded?'

'Of course it's loaded, Mr. Stanno.'

'Well what – I mean. . . .'

'You got a right.'

'Thanks. I know you, don't I?'

'Not very well,' the guy said. He was holding a big black rod in his own paw now, a silenced rod. 'Goodbye, Mr. Stanno.'

He shoved him toward the door. Actually *shoved* Joe Stanno.

The big man staggered into the wall and turned crazed eyes to the smirking silksuited polite bastard. He swiped at his bleeding nose with the back of his hand and growled, 'Where'd you say they were, tough?'

'Same place,' the guy said. 'You'd better get going.'

The guy popped the desk buzzer and the door swung open.

Stanno lurched through the doorway and down the short hall to Max Keno's station. He bent low to whisper, 'What the hell is going on, Max?'

'I'd rather not say, Mr. Stanno,' Max replied.

A cold sweat broke out above Stanno's eyes. It was one thing to get the leper treatment from a stranger . . . Max was something else again. He recoiled from the masked pity in those eyes, then he jerked himself erect and found a handkerchief to hold against the nosebleed.

He took three steps down the stairway before being struck by the eerie silence.

His head jerked around and he gawked across the railing at the deserted tables and the utter desolation of a casino without people. It seemed to Joe the Monster like a Vegas version of the last-man-on-earth.

He snapped back to Max Keno and said, 'God's sake, Max, what's going on?'

'I guess you better just keep on going, Mr. Stanno,' was all Max would say to him.

The red film settled back over his eyes again and Joe Stanno descended into the pits of Mafia hell.

Behind him, faintly, he heard Max calling out, 'It's eightforty, Mr. Vinton.'

CHAPTER SIXTEEN

JACKPOT

Bolan-Vinton strode past Max Keno and said, 'Okay, Max. On me.' He started down the stairway and saw Joe the Monster in his side vision, prowling about the deserted casino.

Bolan kept his eyes front and went on down.

Max fell in behind him.

From behind the partition was coming the muted sounds of a happy party in the adjoining dining-room. That was great. Bolan grinned to himself; the house was living it up, and keeping most of the action where Bolan wanted it.

It was going by the numbers now.

Almost. Just as he reached the casino floor, four men swept in through the lobby entrance.

One of them yelled, 'Hey there!'

Bolan swung around to confront the foursome.

The Talifero brothers, Pat and Mike.

Two tagmen flanking them, running on the quarters like a couple of destroyers in escort of capital vessels.

They were cruising toward Bolan, and they had reached about the midpoint between the door and the stairs. One step around the corner and Bolan would be out of it ... very briefly.

He took a step in their direction, then swung his arm up in a dramatic sweep from the shoulder to point out Joe Stanno, moving like a sleepwalker along a row of gaming tables.

'There he is!' Bolan yelled.

The four came to a confused halt, their eyes tracking along Bolan's point.

Joe Stanno froze and his head snapped up.

The instincts gained by a lifetime of violence were all mirrored there in the big guy, in the street-fight stance, in the way the massive head swayed back to the rear of the shoulders – like a cagey old ostrich laying an eye into the situation.

And the situation he was laying into must have appeared as natural and inevitable to Joe Stanno as any of the hundreds of other similar incidents to which he had been party over the years.

Except that this time Joe Stanno was at the wrong end of the party.

Death ... and eerie silence ... where always before there had been action and at least a synthetic gaiety.

The pointing finger of doom.

And the execution party.

Joe Stanno was obviously having none of that crap. He was not going out bleating and pleading like Vito, hell no.

'Okay, I'll take you all!' he yelled.

Bolan saw him go for his gun, and then he swung quickly away in the other direction and Max Keno scampered in close pursuit.

An excited voice screamed, 'He's crazy!'

The roar of gunfire and the zinging of bullets in confinement accompanied Bolan and his tagman to the rear of the casino. They were passed quickly through the security network, Bolan snarling to the guards, 'It's a rumble, don't let nobody in!'

More money than Bolan knew existed was stacked up all over the joint. Heavily braced wooden shelves along the walls were straining under the burden of thousands upon thousands of coin rolls, and the machines were still ticking.

Currency was stacked in foot-high bundles of four large

counting tables, and the controller, was pacing nervously back and forth and urging the ladies along.

Bolan speared the guy with a hard gaze. 'You got it?' he yelled.

'Yes sir, it's all out. Do I hear gunshots?'

'Every damn nickel?'

'Yes sir, every damn nickel.'

'What are you running, so far?'

'Just over a half-million, Mr. Vinton, but the confirmation count is just going into the—'

'Awright, kill it and get out of here!'

'Sir?'

'There's a rumble, can't you hear? Get your broads outta here, I don't want 'em caught in nothing like this!'

'You mean . . . just leave? Just leave it?'

'You can't take it with you can you, you jerk?' Bolan yelled. 'Get those dames *outta* here!'

It was apparently the final straw for a business-methods freak already pushed beyond the strain-point. The guy spun about and walked stiffly to the door. 'Get them out yourself,' he called over his shoulder, and out he went.

Bolan yelled, 'Leave them doors open! *Out*, girls, *get the hell out*!'

He was grabbing and shoving, and Max was lending a hand to a scene of confusion and pyramiding chaos.

Above the feminine hubbub, Bolan told Max, 'Take 'em out, and make sure they get clear.'

'Sure boss,' said instant loyalty.

And then there was just Bolan and the inside guard. Bolan gave him a hard stare and said, 'Well, are you going down with the bucks?'

The guy said, 'No sir,' and went out.

Bolan went over to the new money, obviously the stuff from the vault, and riffled through the stacks. There were packets of denominations ranging from fifties to thousands. He picked up a packet of the largest denomination and thrust it into his inside coat pocket.

Next he found the fire station and disabled the automatic sprinkler.

And then he went to the door, bent down, produced an incendiary stick he'd been carrying in a leg strap, removed the cap, and tossed the firebomb on to the center table.

It spit and popped and began showering the place with white-hot chemicals, and Bolan got out of there.

The mob was so wild about hot money, he'd give them some. Skim that, he muttered.

He banged the door, ran the combination and commanded the hallway guard, 'Nobody goes in!'

'No *sir*.'

'Not Christ himself! The joint is sealed!'

'I got you, sir.'

He went on through to the casino floor and repeated the command to the two guards there. The guys were nervous and obviously torn up. One of them asked him, 'Did someone try a heist, Mr. Vinton?'

Bolan said, 'Yeh, but don't you worry about the action out front. Just do your job here.'

The guard unholstered his pistol and assured the boss that he would do just that.

Bolan went on around the corner and came out on the main floor. The last of the women were just then disappearing into the dining-room.

Max Keo was returning, skirting warily around the scene of the shooting.

Two guys were laid out on the promenade, bleeding and not moving.

It was hard to tell from the angle of vision, but one of them looked like a Talifero.

Keno yelled, 'Lookout boss! Joe is—'

A gun roared from somewhere in the tables and the little tagman took a dive.

Bolan did likewise, slapping leather in the process, and he came up against a gaming table with the Beretta up and ready.

A bunch of guys ran in from the lobby. Bolan yelled to them, 'Out, get outta here!'

A gun roared again, a bullet splattered into the door moulding, and the guys dodged back to safety.

But Bolan spotted Joe Stanno on that round. He tired along the floor, beneath the tables, the Beretta phutting twice and cutting Stanno's legs from under him.

The monster man went down with a thud and a sigh.

And then the place was being invaded. People were dodging in from both doorways, hard people packing hardware and sprinting for cover wherever cover could be found.

Bolan had but one way to go, and that was toward Joe Stanno. He snaked along the floor beneath the tables where the big guy was lying on his side and watching him come.

Stanno was sieved. He was bleeding from numerous punctures in the chest and one in the gut, a trickle of blood was oozing from the corner of his mouth, and his pants legs were turning red from Bolan's hits.

His gun was lying on the floor, under his nose. He raised his head off the floor and asked Bolan, 'Hey, tough, which one did I get? Was it Pat or Mike?'

'I think you got them both, Joe,' came the reply in Bolan's natural voice.

Joe the Monster smiled and coughed up blood and said, 'I knew they wasn't so tough,' and then he lay his head back down beneath the crap table and died.

A volley of fire hit the table at that precise moment, and Bolan rolled on. From somewhere on his flank he heard Max Keno hissing, 'Boss, what's going on?'

'Bets are off, Max,' he called back. 'You're on yourself.'

Such a situation had apparently never arisen for the little tagman. After a lifetime of forever being 'on' someone else, there was absolutely no mental concept of being 'on himself'.

He snaked and rolled to Bolan's outside flank and gasped, 'Out the kitchen, boss, that's the best way.'

A Taliferi was running down the stairway from the upstairs joint, another guy one step behind. Bolan heard him shouting, 'That's Bolan! Don't let him get out!'

Bolan snapped a Parabellum toward the staircase and he saw the fabric of the Taliferi's suit pop and recoil, and the guy took a nose-dive down the steps.

Someone yelled, *'He hit the boss!'*

Bolan had lost his purple lenses during the scramble, and now Max Keno was staring into his unshuttered eyes with the heady revelation of truth crackling between them. And obviously the truth had no bearing on the matter. The boss was the boss, whatever else he might be. The little guy grinned and chirped, 'Follow me, boss.'

There was no immediate alternative, and Bolan's numbers were running out. He rolled and slid and crawled through the jungle of mahogany and green felt until it began to seem like an eternal trek – and then Max was grunting, 'Go on, straight ahead, I'll cover you.'

Bolan sprang toward a curtain doorway, no more than two table-lengths away. Guns roared and spat – angry little hornets of destruction in hot pursuit, and they were zipping the air all about him, thwacking into the wall beyond and plowing into tables to either side of this back-track. Behind him he could hear Max's methodical response, the air suddenly cleared and the roar of weapons died off.

Also behind him a loud voice was proclaiming, 'We are federal officers! All of you stop firing and throw down your weapons!'

And then Bolan was through the curtains and running along a short hallway and toward a swinging door to the kitchen.

The door swung open and Bolan skidded to an abrupt halt.

Harold Brognola stood there, blocking the way with a sawed-off shotgun raised and ready.

The sad-faced lawman hesitated for perhaps a heartbeat.

And, in that heartbeat, Bolan was aware of a small figure swinging in around him.

Time froze, and Bolan's thoughts raced on, stretching the moment into an infinity of ideas, and he knew that Max Keno, the career tagman, was acting out a subliminal reflex as deeply-rooted as Bolan's own rage for survival, that he was moving his own life into the breach between certain death and 'the boss's' precious body – and little Max Keno died like the true tagman he'd always been.

He took the shotgun charge full in the chest, his pistol firing in reflex, and he was swept back by the blast and flung into the corner of the hallway.

The shotgun clattered to the floor and Brognola sank down with a Keno bullet in the thigh.

Their eyes met and locked momentarily. Bolan threw a regretful and silent farewell to the remains of little Max, and he patted Brognola's shoulder and went on.

Numbers. Never *people*, just the goddamned numbers.

It was beginning to look like a day for lost numbers, however, and the idea was reinforced in Bolan's mind as he swept on into the kitchen. A pile of guys in silk suits were just then pushing in from the dining-room, through a doorway at the far side of the kitchen.

A familiar voice behind Bolan cried, 'Lookout!'

Bolan was throwing a fresh clip into the Beretta, a split-second operation when the chips are down, and he was also throwing himself off the target line in another of those frozen-moment experiences.

The blonde – the Ranger Girl, Miss Badmouth herself – was the owner of the familiar voice, and his side vision was catching her in a mind-jarring and time-freezing expose of slow-motion action frames. She was wearing the same wispy outfit he'd first caught her in and a little nickle-plated revolver was daintily spitting flame from her outstretched hand.

In the front view, the guys at the doorway were wheeling into a rapid reverse and falling back into the dining-room, aided and abetted by the volley of small calibre slugs whizzing into their midst.

Bolan tossed three quick rounds their way to punctuate the withdrawal, and he snared the girl's hand and pulled her along with him to the rear door. The kitchen help were all headed in that direction already – with alacrity – and Bolan merely followed the crowd.

They broke into the fresh air and the girl urgently whispered, 'The desert is your only chance!'

'Not quite,' he muttered, and left her standing there beside a cook in a high white hat as he ran to the corner of the building and started the hand-over-hand climb up the metal ladder to the roof.

The time was 8.59.

Despite everything, right on the numbers.

He thought he could hear the chugging of a rotary-wing craft somewhere in the distance as he gained the roof of the casino.

The girl was coming up the ladder behind him.

He took a moment to tell her, 'Bug off, dammit!'

'I hope you know what you're doing,' she panted. 'Give a girl a hand?'

A commotion on the ground just below made the decision for Bolan. He grabbed her arm and yanked her over the parapet and, in the same motion, sent three rounds phutting down the reverse course.

A pained voice below screamed, 'Oh shit!' and a volley of fire tore into the parapet.

The roof was flat, in typical desert style, and broken only by the small superstructure of 'Vito's joint', which had been so painstakingly emplaced there by a man of caution, about halfway to the street end of the building. The rest of the roof was open range and plenty large enough for a whirly-bird to nest upon.

Someone was standing in a darkened window of the adjacent hotel, at about the third floor level and just across the roof from Bolan's position. Two, three, some-ones. Bolan was trying to keep an eye on them, protect his rear at the ladder, and watch for the helicopter all at once.

He told the girl, 'Thanks for the assist, but I wish—'

She swung in behind him and Bolan heard her little pistol biting on empty chambers. He whirled and put a nine-millimeter marker on the forehead of a guy peering up over the roof parapet. The guy disappeared with a grunt.

Toby gasped, 'Do I hear a helicopter?'

He muttered, 'I sure hope you do.'

And then the little humming-bird swung in out of the darkness and reflected the neon glare from the strip. The guys at the hotel window had spotted it also, and they'd spotted the pair on the roof, as well. People were shifting around over there, and Bolan caught the glint of a rifle barrel emerging from the window. He unloaded the Beretta in a rapidfire at the window just as the little bird came to a hover above him.

A rope ladder tumbled down. Bolan grabbed it and pulled the girl over and told her, 'Go!'

She shook her head and said, 'This is where I bug off. God luck, swinger. We'll cross again.'

He took a second away from his precious numbers to give her a stare, and then he knew.

He said, 'It's your dice, honey,' and he quickly ascended the rope ladder.

'Move it!' he yelled when he was halfway up, reinforcing the command with a wave of his hand.

And then they were going straight up and slipping away over the desert, and the glare of the neon jungle was falling off and diminishing, and it all looked so small and insignificant now.

And, of course, it was.

EPILOGUE

'You said nine o'clock,' the pilot reminded him, yelling to be heard above the racket of the rotors. 'Was that close enough?'

'It was plenty close enough,' Bolan yelled back.

Yeah. Plenty close enough.

It had been quite a fling at Vegas.

Carl Lyons, he hoped, would be alive and well because of that fling.

A bit of rot, here and there, had been surgically removed from the American swing scene. It would, of course, grow right back ... but a guy had to keep trying.

He'd met some nice people along the way. And left some.

He hoped that Hal Brognola wouldn't feel too badly over his failure, and somehow, Bolan knew that he would not.

He'd gained a new insight into the lesser men behind the guns. Lesser? No. Bolan would never forget little Max Keno.

As far as the Taliferi ... he hoped they'd found enough blood to wash their hands with ... but he did not particularly care one way or the other. It was their vendetta, not his. He would not go so far as to scratch them out of his combat book ... he'd thought them dead before and been proven wrong.

Tommy Anders, the hottest ethnologist in the land, now *there* was a guy. Bolan hoped that he would not retire from the soul biz of America.

As for the blonde ... Bolan was feeling a bit upset over that item. All the while she'd been. ... What? Where did she fit? Fed? Was she working with Lyons? Was Anders part of the game?

He sighed over the memory of her, knowing that she was a gal who could care for herself . . . but he had to wonder what she was *really* like. She'd been playing a role. Probably as much a role as Bolan's Vinton routine. Would they cross trails again?

It figured that they would. Official people had a way of popping in and out at irregular intervals along Bolan's wipe-out trail. It was a small combat world.

And now . . . where was he headed? Where did the trail lead from here?

He inspected the uneasy face of the accountant, huddled in the rear seat with his bags of bucks.

'San Juan?' Bolan yelled at him.

The guy blinked his eyes and gave Bolan a scared nod.

'That's great,' Bolan yelled, 'because I'm riding shotgun all the way?'

The guy nodded again and looked away.

Bolan relaxed and settled into his seat.

Vegas was nothing now but a glow across the horizon. They were running low, skimming beneath any possible radar search. The little air buggy did not have much range, but Bolan knew there would be another wing waiting somewhere out there, warmed and ready to lift them on to the merry-go-round in the Caribbean. There were times when Bolan could appreciate the mob's efficiency.

And he was looking forward to that ride. Bolan had never grabbed a brass ring . . . the Caribbean carousel sounded like a good place to try.

No brass rings at Vegas, but . . . if nothing else, he'd done something that probably a million guys had dreamed of doing all their lives. He'd gone to Vegas, beat the house at their own game, and cleaned out the bank. Ashes to ashes and dust to . . .

He grinned, remembering.

Destiny's Dice had turned out to be loaded . . . against the house, for a change. And the wipe-out trail was growing longer by the moment, wasn't it? There just might be a hot reception awaiting him at the end of this particular segment.

He lit a cigarette, and slowly blew out the smoke, examined his soul, and found it intact. 'San Juan,' he murmured, 'here we come.'

THE END

THE EXECUTIONER: ARIZONA AMBUSH
by DON PENDLETON

Bolan's new challenge—beat the devil himself in Arizona . . .

Hinshaw . . . Worthy . . . Morales . . . names with ghostly echoes from Mark Bolan's military past. Add to these an abandoned combat training centre in the Arizona wasteland, a kinky U.S. Senator, a badly soiled businessman, a self-exiled Mafia chieftain with new territorial ambitions, and a bunch of combat veterans . . . and it means war in the desert for the Executioner . . . Arizona, the land of sun and sand, is transformed overnight into the bloody dunes of the damned as Bolan once again closes in on the enemy and paradise becomes the Devil's Playground.

0 552 10830 8 65p

EXECUTIONER 24: CANADIAN CRISIS
by DON PENDLETON

Sydicates from all over the world were moving into Montreal. The occasion? An international underground congress to discuss the formation of the Costa di tutti Cosi – the most formidable crime network ever envisaged . . . Quebec was already smouldering with French nationalist sentiment – if the smoke fanned into revolution, Quebec would fall like a plum into the hands of the mob . . . With relations between Canada and the USA in jeopardy, energy resources threatened and world powers on the brink of disaster, Bolan came to Canada – with his own particular brand of hell-fire . . .

0 552 10457 4 60p

NO ORCHIDS FOR MISS BLANDISH
by JAMES HADLEY CHASE

When Dave Fenner was hired to solve the Blandish kidnapping, he knew the odds were against him – the cops were still looking for the girl three months after the ransom had been paid. And the kidnappers, Riley and his gang, had disappeared into thin air. But what none of them knew was that Riley had been wiped out by a rival gang – and the heiress was now in the hands of Ma Grisson and her son Slim, a vicious killer who couldn't stay away from women . . . especially his beautiful new captive. By the time Fenner began to close in on them, some terrible things had happened to Miss Blandish . . .

0 552 10522 8 60p

THE SUCKER PUNCH
by JAMES HADLEY CHASE

Chad Winters was a small-time bank clerk – until he was put in charge of the Shelley account. Vestal Shelley was plain, a bitch . . . and worth over seventy million dollars. No one had ever dared stand up to her before – but Chad, determined to get his hands on her money, found the perfect way to treat her . . . and ended up as her husband. But he hadn't reckoned on falling violently in love with Vestal's secretary – a ruthless woman who also wanted her share of the fortune . . . and who cunningly turned Chad's thoughts to murder . . .

0 552 10575 9 65p